And Your Point Is?

Scorn and Meaning in Jeff Lint's Fiction

Steve Aylett's other books are

Slaughtermatic

Atom

Toxicology

Only an Alligator

The Velocity Gospel

Dummyland

Karloff's Circus

The Crime Studio

Bigot Hall

The Inflatable Volunteer

Fain the Sorcerer

Shamanspace

LINT

And Your Point Is?

Scorn and Meaning in Jeff Lint's Fiction

edited by Steve Aylett

Published by Raw Dog Screaming Press,
Hyattsville, MD

Paperback Edition

Cover image: Jennifer C. Barnes
Book design: John Edward Lawson

Printed in the United States of America

ISBN 978-1-933293-17-2

Library of Congress Control Number: 2006935191

www.rawdogscreaming.com

'Thuds from a grave: a good thing?'
—Jeff Lint, *Fanatique*

'Genuine creativity will, by definition, result in something new and never seen before. But despite people's claims that they welcome or crave originality, their dislike of the new and unfamiliar means that any encounter with real creativity will always send them scampering away—perhaps giggling nervously like tarts, at best.'
—Jeff Lint, Interview, 1970

'I find both naively charming and horrifying the constant emphasis on postmodern subjectivity in our modern world, while those authorities who encourage and profit by that trend in the populace privately covet the hard facts.'
—Alfred Bork, '"Deep Vanishing" in Jeff Lint's Science Fiction'

Contents

Introduction

JEFF LINT SAID in interview that many authors' creation of 'understandable' characters who are a kind of 'hollow' each reader was supposed to occupy, soon left him aggravated as a reader: 'I will want to turn left and the character will turn right; I would ignore but the character obeys; I would destroy an argument but the character is blandly convinced and wastes years of his life. As a reader I find myself locked within an automaton I cannot control, which will never do what I would do (even by chance), and which provides no nourishment.' Lint's idea of an acceptable hero was a spider with multiple eyes like rally car headlights who, when issued an order, would jet tears of mirth from the entire bank of eyes and tell a friend later while adapting a submarine for spaceflight: 'I hadn't the heart to obey such a moron.'

Alfred Bork has called Lint's writing 'pointillist' and I think this derives from the fact that every single sentence comes directly at you. Each point is the head of a thread, a retrievable plumb-line of information. But few have taken up the option to draw on such threads. Critics who momentarily subjected themselves to the rigors of Lint's flaying, vortical screeds would quickly withdraw and resort to condemning books such as *Jelly Result* for being 'made up from beginning to end,' an argument which required such a faux-jaded powering-down of their own faculties that the energy required to advance it could barely be mustered.

It seems Lint's day was incomplete until he had scavenged the treasure-trove of truths discarded by fashion as worthless, arranged them into meaning swarms (a practice similar to bit torrenting but utilizing revolutions miniaturized to the size of full-sized ones' effectiveness) and tricked out the interior with ingeniously embedded lights, dragon glass and characters who 'interrupt the world' with a cough of honesty at the least convenient moment. No doubt is left that Earth is circling the drain. Sunlight dawns without realization—it's always the same light. Enough of this hammering can turn the untrained head into undifferentiated dissent goop, a sort of sub-resentment squantum which may result in you blurting aloud on the bus 'so *I'm* the eel in this equation.' There are passages where Lint has clearly decided it wouldn't be a bad idea to live as an undisturbed cobweb on the moon or as a mudfish, gelid and pulsating. A premonition or a preview? He seems to have anticipated the unlivable conditions humanity would soon attain.

So much has been written elsewhere about Lint's novels (not least in my own book *LINT*) that I've mostly chosen pieces which deal with his shorter fiction. These writers and journalists should be applauded for tackling Lint's work because, damn.

—Steve Aylett

'The Retrial'

Steve Aylett

JEFF LINT'S INTERPRETATION of Kafka's *The Trial* was that the guilt felt by K—and depended upon by the state—derives from his having allowed the state to become so powerful in the first place. K therefore ultimately accepts his punishment.

In Lint's story 'The Retrial' K feels no such guilt because he allows no such influence and storms into every circumstance like a berserk Touretter, somehow spanning the most chasmic beartraps by sheer velocity of mischief.

Lint's K is a classic Lintian hero—individual to the point of parallel-dimensionality. In his novel *Jelly Result* Lint would portray the maintenance of oppression by automated human patch-and-repair, those dependent systems simultaneously and constantly preying on the life force of its maintainers. This is Lint's idea of hell and he revels in the hero's disengagement from it. His attempt at an Asimovian short, 'The Robot Who Couldn't Be Bothered' portrays a robot whose apparently faulty inactivity is discovered to be the result of 'eleven million nodes of personal consideration.' The entire second half of the novel *I Am a Centrifuge* is taken up with a volley of justified sarcasm so detailed and complete as to have its own visible lungs and nervous system. The hero in Lint's story 'Bless' awakes one morning to find that he has no tentacles. Alarmed, he dashes out to discover that nobody else has any tentacles either and all claim in bafflement never to have had any. As Michael Hersh has observed, the metaphor points up 'a moral or ethical sensibility which, unheld and unrecognized by anyone else on the planet, is not communicable.' In most Lint stories this sensibility is that of honesty and independent thought.

In 'The Retrial' Joseph K visits the zoo one morning to be greeted by two warders, Franz and Willem, who tell him he's under arrest. He laughs good-naturedly, asking to see their underwear. They refuse, and this lack of reciprocity—their assumption that he must obey their commands while they need not obey his—is what seems to spark K's apparently uncooperative attitude. An Inspector is stood scowling nearby but since no introduction or instruction is given and all is left to some unspoken assumption, K begins to shudder in place like a dodgy steam tank, his convulsions building as though toward some terrible outburst. At the apex his head sags like a bag, splitting to release precisely eleven scorpions onto the ground. K himself collapses like a rotted scarecrow and soon, kicked and scattered by the fleeing crowd, is no longer really in evidence. He is at the court, kicking the outer wall of the Usher's cabin. "'I'm naked," he thought, almost amazed: "First being born, and now this. No trousers for me."' When grabbed by K the Usher sees that the complicated epaulets on K's shoulders are actually the skulls of rabbits. He pleads with K to get off, that he has his own troubles, but K is adamant about doing what he sees as his duty. Finally four under-ushers try to pull them both out of the cabin but are foiled. The scene cuts to what appears to be several days later, as the Usher lays inert amid a jumble of steaming wreckage. There is a strange slamming sound as the Usher's eyes start open.

Thus begins a course of what Jean-Marie Guerin has called

'ecstatic disregard' in relation to memo-level fascism: 'Without this undercurrent of beatific irreverence it is impossible to pin down Lint's Joseph K's complete lack of need or desire to become involved with the processes of oppression. It should be noted also that the "berserk stenographer" style in which Lint relates the story is important in allowing these situations to actually appear less philosophically interesting than they are.'

Lint's K tells the story 'Beside the Law' in which a man from the country comes to the door seeking admittance to the Law, but the guard says he can't come in now. So the man constructs a precise replica of the door and locates it beside the first one, placing a sign above it for '$20 a blowjob' and waiting for trade, which is brisk. Finally, when the guard at the first door is about to die, he asks why people stopped coming to his door. 'That door could be profitable only for you,' the man from the country says. 'And now I'm going to close it.'

Like Kafka's K, Lint's has a mind of his own, but unlike that K, he has a breathtaking intuition for the lateral response: a sort of laser-guided effrontery. When asked where he was on a particular evening, K replies: 'Well, I'll tell you—if you have any money?' Outraged, the Magistrate's response is cut short by his perceiving what seems to be a mere sheaf of undulating bacon fibers where K had previously been standing.

Anyone who has actually broken official protocol will know that at best it sends its agents into a sort of contentless whirl which does not have the vibrancy of honest panic, nor even that of genuine surprise— they seem merely to swerve from familiar bureaucratic rails onto some of the minor, less used branches of evasion. Nothing is ever changed, admitted or learnt. Yet in the world of 'The Retrial' some effect can be had; perhaps by the sheer diagonal intensity of K's responses. Consider the cathedral scene—while you or I might merely windmill our arms and puff our cheeks out a bit, K delivers a roundhouse to the priest by detonating into a perfumed cloud of dandelion seeds and buff-colored smoke. The priest, who had been 'smiling like a warship' only seconds before, now crouches on the floor like a spider, 'karking and keening'—he seems to have been both deafened and confused by the blast.

Recent critics have suggested that the satirical accesses of Lint heroes are a result of intense tetraneutron activity, supposedly explaining their combination of precision and apparent chaos. Hypercomplex satire operates by applying social rules in the 'wrong' contexts such as those of logic, morality or honesty, and the four-prong tetraneutron cluster (the four neutrons of which will arrive simultaneously if fired at a carbon target) would seem the perfect structure for it—all the more entertainingly so as the phenomena's existence is doubted. If you tweak the laws of physics to allow four neutrons to bind together, all kinds of chaos ensues (*Journal of Physics*, vol 29, L9). It would mean that the mix of elements formed after the big bang was inconsistent with what most people now believe and, even worse, the matter created would be far too heavy for the current model to cope.

The theory stated in Lint's story 'Death by Fred' is that 'sabotage is best accomplished by channeling bad luck.' In Lint, until you're an individual, you're not in contention. This is why Lint could never write about the sort of characters that appeared in other people's books. Almost every scene has a sort of surreal exultation to it.

At the moment his case is due to be heard, K is watching the lions at the zoo, his eyes full of tears. Two men approach and, their arms entwined with his on either side of him, begin to walk him through the city. K begins smiling, the grin seeming to become broader than his face. Finally they arrive at an abandoned quarry. The two men take out a butcher knife and begin passing it to each other in a threatening manner. He is apparently supposed to take it and plunge it into himself. But without aid of the knife a red ace of hearts blooms at his chest and spreads quickly to stain his entire body and head. He has become a pillar of blood in the shape of a man, which soon becomes semi-transparent. It fades until only his Cheshire-cat grin remains, a miniature sunset which whispers echoing as it disappears: 'Like a god!'

Sources:
Cheerful When Blamed—Jeff Lint (Rich & Cowan, 1957)
The Trial—Franz Kafka
'The Bartleby Stance'—Simon Posford (*The Lintian* #7, 1995)
'Belligerently Naked in Jeff Lint's "The Retrial"'—Jean-Marie Guerin (*Journal of Vortical Literature*, Issue 13, 1997)
'Inconvenience From Outer Space'—Michael H. Hersh (*Sensurround Blame Magazine*, Issue 14, 1985)

Review of
I am a Centrifuge

Eileen Welsome

A TRUE HERO, one who completely satisfies our sense of independence, is a hero who is elsewhere. This hero may not, necessarily, spring from a self-reliance background. *Jelly Result*'s Valac is certainly not the child of interesting parents. However, he, like many of Lint's characters, is a person who harbors no illusions about fashion or its importance.

Certainly, Lint has created a number of characters who are less than clever. Bobb Watts, of *Turn Me Into a Parrot*, is a moron. Alger Lattimore of the play *The Coffin Was Labelled Benjy the Bear* is a hen-riding, easily-surprised fool. Yet these characters, clearly, are humorous devices designed to heighten a sense of bafflement in the reader. (The story somehow proceeds in such a way that the characters create the same effects and changes that a properly-appointed Lint hero would.) The real Lint hero, the one who appeals to us most, is irreverent to the point of parallel-dimensionality; despite a life of lurid extremity in surroundings such as a Dog-Angering Factory, or toil in a mine where gas is his only friend, the Lint protagonist will enter the tale wearing

17

neon pants which seem to get bigger throughout his adventures, until eventually the other characters must acknowledge them, and finally deal with them as the primary threat to their survival ('The Rustic Intensity of Benny's Truss'). Gender is no barrier to this syndrome; Isou of *Slogan Love*, one of Lint's few central female characters, is a study in casual scorn and cosmically preoccupied unavailability, all external manipulation meeting empty air.

It is hard to find a character that fits this mold better than Surge Brunner of *I am a Centrifuge*. Standing amid a society that mimics personal power and 'choice' above all, he can barely draw breath for laughing—while the constant allowances he must make while moving through this vacuum of dishonesty has forced the bones of his head to bulge out sideways like a faulty vase. In a way, he is using his own skull as a sort of space helmet.

Unlike Felix Arkwitch of *The Stupid Conversation*, whose deeds are quietly epic and ignored, Surge represents that variety of hero whose rarity and weakness derives from the fact that he is an unshakably honest and humorous man. Though the society surrounding him is toxic, with the concepts of right and wrong non-synchronizedly transposed so many times at so minute a level as to be shredded, he calmly irons his pants with a warm armadillo. In Lint's stories it is through such a hero that we derive a sense of moral grounding.

Much is expected of Surge, as he is worked, taxed and exhausted like everyone else. For Surge, this is especially poignant, as he has been fully aware of all that has been done to him, every second of his life from the start. This hypersensitivity, which the refreshingly colorful Doctor Webb terms 'common sense' causes such problems for Surge that he chooses to stay at the middling pain level of his home for much of the time. Emerging into society, Surge will sometimes begin screaming, grabbing people and staring them in the eye point-blank as the flesh begins to drool from his face.

More to the point is that seeing the underpinnings of the world at all times, he finds himself to be terribly frank and unpopular wherever he goes. People greet him only to receive a series of ugly shocks, or badinage of such grotesque extremity that some find their ribs have turned to a fine powder within their chests. (Many such characters subsequently die believing that they have been shot by a fab new weapon). As it turns out, the centuries of exploited existence have changed the very meaning of happiness. Eroding definitions (or in this accelerated world, redefining by bland decree) is a queasy sport which Lint called Memerade. Openly, blithely and uselessly contemptuous of the society contemporary to his lifespan, Surge achieves nothing except simple and absolute faith to himself.

And so the stage is set. What follows is the typical Lintian combination of obtusely-timed lethargy and pyrotechnical misbehavior that characterize his writings. Lint's presentation of defiance is rich and complex. At a gala luncheon at which the President will speak, things are tense. Surge is mostly a gentle fellow, rarely moved to hostility or violence. However, the sense of anticipation deriving from the knowledge that he will presently begin to shudder and shout, clenched teeth showing through a face streaming like hot wax, functions as the proverbial 'bomb under the table.' It might be said that, of all Lint's social inventions, the Lintian act of effrontery is the most fascinating and elaborate.

Sometimes, these are merely alluded to in the course of a story as a background incident which gives us an idea of a character's likes and dislikes (eg. Barry Soylent's car-torching in *Clowns & Locusts*). Elsewhere they are volleys of sarcasm so elaborate as to constitute dramatic productions (eg. Lashpool's forty-seven-page chicken theatre outburst at the dinner party in *Die Miami*). In *Centrifuge*, however, Lint takes special pains to elevate a lazily disdainful bit of jeering to the level of masterpiece, providing it with a highly developed structure of levels, phases and movements. The reader of the second half of *Centrifuge* is witness to a renunciation blow-out, played from start to finish with intricate play by play detail. Through a seemingly trivial remark by another guest, the exponential eruption of Surge's mockery is a deceptively impressive feat and an amazing example of Lint's level of concentration and dedication to his stories.

Respect for others acts as connecting thread throughout the first half of *Centrifuge*. It is a trait of the docile Surge that he gives people the credit to assess, accept or disregard his acts and remarks. But in true Lintian fashion the outgoing thread of respect tangles with threads of manipulation and dishonesty coming the other way; the knot created finally becomes such an obstruction to Surge's peace that he must explode into a nova of derision to burn it away.

Like *Doomed & Confident* and countless other Lint novels, *I am a Centrifuge* gives us a glimpse of honesty which sparks briefly within a society very like our own, before being snuffed again by the vacuum.

Clearly it's no mean feat for an author to fill half of a good-sized novel with a stream of intricately-demonstrated verbal abuse but Lint makes it a fertile paradise of colors, giving Surge's logic an entire anatomy including bellowing lungs which, like all good satire, are powered by the flawed arguments of its target. The guests, for some time frozen like deer in the headlights, eventually attempt to escape but find the ballroom closed off by their own assertion that Surge has nothing to do but tolerate their dismal company. (This and a couple of other elements have been compared to Stephen King's *Carrie*, which was published the same year).

Finally the visible twists and clots of manipulation are hanging in the air over the shrieking assembly and dripping noxious slurry upon all. But Surge has efforted so much beyond himself that, when he incinerates the terrible mass in mid-air, he destroys the mechanism of complex truth within him. Something in him is also purified away and he is left a simpleton, unable to explain himself or anything else. The bedraggled guests stagger from the building in a daze, including a wealthy dowager whose mouth has disappeared. The evening's vortex becomes an urban myth, of course.

The concept of Surge's long-contained eruption is a perfect Lintian excuse for mischief. In the early Random publication of *I Am a Centrifuge*, the cover art offers us an interesting representation of Surge blowing some kind of galaxy out of his ass. Behind him are primly affronted characters representing the gala guests, some of them throwing their entire arms across their eyes (which seems excessive). Though an inaccurate representation, anyone who saw the cover and who knew Lint's work, should have suspected at once that he was the creator of *Centrifuge*, as opposed to Alan Rouch, whose name first graced the cover. Rouch's *Sadly Disappointed*, on the other hand, is an average sort of a book to which Rouch has added a few hens in the hope of seeming 'wacky.' Though misguided in swapping books with his friend Rouch, Lint should be given credit for trying to help out the lesser author.

EDITOR's NOTE:
I am a Centrifuge, published under Alan Rouch's name in 1974, is generally agreed to have been written by Jeff Lint.

Around the same time, the would-be 'demonic possession' thriller *Sadly Disappointed* was published under the name Isaac Asimov, the implication being that it was written by Lint. Alan Rouch has since admitted to writing that piece of garbage.

Redemption & Ordeal in Jeff Lint's 'Broadway Crematoria'

Arkhipov Halt

THE BIBLE'S NOTION of the 'promised land' has been deemed a serviceable concept in literature. Modern authors reinterpret this biblical ideal to include an exasperating variety of redemptions, salvations and sanctuaries. This is an important concept in Lint's story 'Broadway Crematoria.' The story focuses on the protagonist's sense of claustrophobia until the moment of deliverance. Thus, whether his deliverance is mental or physical, the protagonists' salvation lies ultimately in a sense of spatial freedom.

'Broadway Crematoria' begins with a corrupted ideal of death as a time of redemption. Lenny visits the Broadway Funeral Home because he has inadvertently killed a shopgirl; he is sent away by the fierce proprietor to fetch the body. Parallels can be drawn between Lenny and the biblical Judas, who also must take responsibility for a certain death he would rather forget. When Lenny returns with the body in a sack, he is greeted by a furtive midget: 'a sudden access of mirth ended the man's whisperings, so that Lenny was all the more bored.' However, a crucial difference between the biblical betrayal and Lint's is that, despite its horror, the latter sends Lenny on a fun jape, however brief this proves to be. He keeps in his pocket the stolen trinket which he believes to be a rare pearl, and thinks he has something going for him. He mashes the midget's face against the plush carpet of the vestibule, and screams with laughter.

Despite this detail, 'Broadway Crematoria' remains a tale of redemption: 'Lenny was wearing polo-neck pants, yes siree. They'd never get him alive.' This image suggests that America, the Land of Freedom, may also be Lenny's House of Bondage. Judas has a similar experience—he escapes the authorities (who are in fact not interested in him) and advances only to fall into the clutches of a madness he has been nurturing with nougat and turkish delight for years. After his death he becomes an important figure in Israel, Egypt and environs for playing a part in one of the big stories of the age. Lenny too goes unknowingly into a new land which may prove the antithesis of the Promised Land he thought it to be. His alienation is underscored in biblical terminology. He describes himself as 'a natural man among plastic saints' as Moses refers to himself as 'a stranger in a strange land.' (*Exodus 2:22*)

Despite his idealized expectations of the funeral parlor, no doubt stemming from the conception of America at the time as the land of opportunity, Lenny discovers a place of accusation, insinuation and lethargy. At first, under the instructions of the Head Funerer, he rolls the body in blue wax, feeling well received and safe. But even then, he begins to be claustrophobic. In fact, before going to sleep that first night in a back room, he finds himself 'squeezed uncomfortably' under the stoker's bunk. It is through this physical oppressiveness that Lenny makes his first personal connection, with the crematorium's stoker. This friendship soon disintegrates as Lenny tries to entertain the stoker with a sort of sock puppet, which the stoker believes is supposed to represent himself. Despite his arrival at the funerers as a customer, Lenny is almost a prisoner. His only contact with the city outside the funeral parlor is the view directly up the furnace chimney, but he is kept from enjoying this pleasure by his duties in cleaning the interior; the stoker 'frowned with annoyance if he ever found Lenny craning up at the distant circle of sky.'

The first time Lenny tries to escape the funeral parlor he trips over the now dead body of the midget and, folding under the Master's implication that the death resulted from Lenny's previous face-pressed-to-carpet attack, he finds he must destroy the body himself. As a diabolical test, he is given only a fork and a safety match with which to achieve the disposal. It is here that Lenny feels most overwhelmed by his claustrophobic surroundings. The building itself is oppressive. The Master Funerer says, "'Don't you find that one gets a kind of free feeling on coming out of the stoking room into the casket display area?"…"He talks," thought Lenny, "as if he knew nothing about this huge house, the endless corridors, the chapel, the empty rooms, the darkness everywhere."' But it is not just the labyrinth of dark corridors that contributes to Lenny's claustrophobia: 'everything cramped him here.' He is attacked by the stoker, to the point where he sees him 'as a deliverer.' He is psychologically tricked by his host when the Master Funerer questions him: 'You don't need both eyes do you?' When they are done talking, Lenny finds that the Master has his arm tightly around him, 'and involuntarily he struggled to free himself from the long arm.' He envisions a clear but impossible escape: 'down the corridor, down the other hallway, through the furnace room, across the display chamber, down the steps, across the foyer, through that glass door, down the stoop, through the streets, through the suburbs, along the country roads to the great world of trees and singing birds and naked women so smooth you could slide down them.'

And Your Point Is?

However, once Lenny has disposed of the midget, his success leads him to more oppression and labor comparable to slavery. He finds that he must serve tea and cakes to the stoker and Master Funerer, as well as a mysterious man known only as 'Rameses,' a trial that shares its hardship with the Israelites while in bondage in Egypt: 'And they made their lives bitter with hard bondage, in mortar, and in brick, and in all manner of service in the field: all their service, wherein they made them serve, was with rigor.' (*Exodus 1:11-14*) Lenny describes his haughty superiors with similar narrative force. He is shocked by the intensity of the work: 'he had had no conception of such work as this.' 'After a twelve-hour shift at the furnace, coming off duty at six o'clock in the morning, he was so weary that he dreamed of going straight to bed without heeding anyone. But he must don his maids garments and serve cupcakes on a silver tray, keeping his head always bowed beneath a bonnet.' The grueling work contributes to Lenny's progressive sense of enclosure and alienation. When he tries a second time to escape the funeral parlor, he finds himself trapped once again in a compromising position as he confronts a grieving customer and pretends to be a sort of mannequin. Dishevelled and covered in soot, he explains in a mechanized voice that he is intended to represent the condition that a loved one can expect to be in after the cremation process. After the customers leave in disgust, Lenny knows from his previous mistakes that he will be punished like the lowest dog: 'he flinched in an involuntary but unsuccessful attempt to escape his own imaginings.' In the event, he is placed inside a casket with eleven baby chicks for nine days. Upon finding that Lenny has not surrendered to the urge to eat any of the birds, the Master Funerer regards Lenny as less than human.

Thus, instead of sanctuary, the funeral parlor has become Lenny's land of bondage from which he must escape. His escape mirrors the biblical Exodus in its dramatic composition. Lenny follows a mouse to a small chink in the storeroom wall through which a draft blows. Peering through the chink, Lenny is confronted with the face of a clown who is calling for staff in the World Free Circus, claiming, 'Everyone is welcome! ... Our circus can find employment for everyone, a place for everyone!' Lenny notes that even 'destitute, disreputable characters' are hired. In the biblical exodus, Moses also insists on everyone's inclusion. He will not even accept Pharaoh's offer to let all but the cattle go. The Israelites leave Egypt in a hurry; they cannot take anything with them, or even wait for their bread to rise. Lenny notes that 'all I'll take is the pearl,' the strange, seamed gem he stole from the shopgirl. He piles caskets around the open furnace door and begins a massive conflagration, then runs through the foyer swinging a shovel.

The dramatization of the hiring process recalls more biblical significance. The Israelites, like the putative employee of the World Free Circus, have no concept of where they are going, but trust in the unknown promised land. Lenny's excitement is underscored by a long-awaited release from the confines of his previous life in the Broadway Funeral Home. 'Only now did Lenny understand how huge America was.' The street Lenny crosses on his way to the Circus hiring office holds new promise. Clutching the pearl, Lenny finds that even the confines of the waiting room cannot take away his newfound feeling of freedom: 'Everything that went on in the little room, which was thick with cigarette-smoke in spite of the open window, faded into comparative insignificance before the grandeur of the world outside.' Mental images of wide-open landscapes abound in the story's penultimate scene. Thus we expect Lenny to find in the promise of the Free World the land of redemption his recent experiences in the funeral parlor did not offer.

The interview office itself presents a similarly claustrophobic environment in which the wide-open landscapes of Lenny's imaginings fold and collapse before the gaze of three clowns, who immediately unmask to reveal their identity as the stoker, the Master Funerer and the sinister Rameses. Laughing with ease, Rameses takes the pearl from Lenny and places it on the desk, all three men leaning toward it. When the Master Funerer begins prying minutely at the pearl, Lenny bolts up and leaves the room. A massive explosion shreds the building as Lenny leaps from the fire escape.

Lenny attains spatial freedom from his claustrophobic life. Of course, we cannot be sure that Broadway or the open country will be the promised land Lenny expects, since Lint leaves Lenny literally in mid-air, but the imagery of limitless landscapes that we are left with suggests that Lenny's quest will soon come to fruition. Like the Jews leaving Egypt, Lenny leaves a land of slave labor for unknown but promising territory.

References:
Mask of Disapproval—Jeff Lint (Rich & Cowan, 1961)
'*Phantasm*, the Tall Man and Broadway Crematoria: Jeff Lint's Influence on Modern Horror' by John Drick (*CineLit*, Vol IV Issue 5)
'Must I Speak of it Again'—by Cameo Herzog (collected in *Dust We Shall Become: Collected Reviews of Cameo Herzog*—Balkan Books, 1969)

Give, Take and Take:
An examination of Jeff Lint's 'The Crystalline Associate' (collected in *Lint: a Collection*)

Daniel Guyal

A FAST-MOVING political thriller, a lament for the world's purported creative ideals that blends the baffled with the bitterly angry, a coruscating story of betrayal that burrows deep into the roots of human history, the nature of the divine, and ultimately of reality itself—'The Crystalline Associate' is none of these. It also lacks the gill-blazing heroes of Lint's novels. But in the non-stop tilling of jaded heresies to find something actually interesting and the showcasing of 'billions-will-run-a-circuit-of-the-earth-to-avoid it' genuine originality it's pure Lintage.

Before discussing the nature of the story's strengths—and its, to my mind, weaknesses—it is necessary to give a brief summary of the content, though such summary can only be a pale parody of a plot that flits and crackles like a burning bird.

The book has eleven narrators, none of whom play a part in the action, as they are bears at the zoo and observe the two main characters from behind bars. Joseph Holbrooke is first seen chuffed and grateful with his literary agent, an amicable man who promises Joe great things for the future. However, upon several subsequent visits Joe is alone. Later he is seen whining to his girlfriend about the absent agent, whom he describes as having ossified into a kind of crystalline statue. 'He's not only brittle and immobile but workshy. He doesn't flinch or respond to my jibes or entreaties, Mary. I don't believe there's any life in him at all. What use is that to me?' Joe demands of the timid girl. '*Why* is he doing this to me?'

When next seen, Joe is alone again. He has with him a towel which he unrolls to reveal a hand which looks as if it's made of boiled candy. 'What do you make of that?' he asks a passing dog, which unexpectedly snaps at the treat and, after an arduous (and very detailed) tug-of-war, wrests it away from the outraged author.

'I was going to have that tested at the Institute,' he shouts after the mutt. He continues to shout an intricate theory after the vanished dog, acquainting us with several possible explanations for the agent's condition, all building up to his favorite, 'carapace redux.' This rock-like state is in fact the normal condition for the creature—and the mobile and active version was the aberration. 'Just as insects and other animals may do impressions of each other for personal gain.' But what did this stone creature gain from its very brief masquerade as a human agent? At this point Joe stops yelling after the vanished dog and decides to sit down, by which point an Irish cop has arrived. A farcical scene ensues where Joe says that the dog bit his hand and so on, the comically puzzled cop finds no wound on Joe's hands, and Joe finds he must lash out at the officer with both arms and legs, an uncoordinated display which has the cop laughing even as he is injured. Joe runs away and the bears silently watch him go.

One night the bears are awoken by a disturbance beyond the bars—Joe has vaulted the zoo walls and brought with him an unwieldy

sack which he up-ends on a wooden seat to reveal a candied and inert
version of the agent we saw in the first scene. The thing looks 'pupaic'
or as though made of cheap colored glass. The head has become
blackened and clouded, and one hand looks to have been sawed off.
Joe berates the thing for vampirizing his hopes while banking forever
on his gratitude, a process he calls 'hostaging to the future.' He pours
gasoline over the crystalline parasite and sets it ablaze. As the creature
blackens and melts, a ghostly etheric artery snakes from the effigy
to Joe, through which his power returns. Joe begins flipping out,
whooping at the sky and juddering on the spot. The agent creature
burns on—there seems to be something like a real human skull within
the drooling head.

This is an extremely bare bones account, basically, of the 'surface
events'—so wherein lie the tremendous strengths, and the notable
flaws?

Flaws: for one—the fight scene with the dog. Joe and the dog pull
back and forth, each trying to free the ossified hand from the other.
The struggle lasts nearly four pages in the Phair edition of *Lint: a
Collection* and I believe it derives from a rare instance of Lint padding
for the pulps (the story originally appeared in *Why?* magazine).

Second—the fight with the cop. Joe leaves the cop alive, a
forbearance which dates the tale terribly.

Consternation may also result from Lint's description of the
girlfriend Mary as 'an elongated owl in a crimson coat' and her habit
of constantly whistling along to the tune of what people are saying.
(However, I love it and crave to meet such a woman.)

One of the greatest strengths lies in the almost extra-sensory,
triangulated perception established by the onlooking bears, through
whom we view the story. The bears have furry fun comparing and
contrasting each 'Joe Show,' shuffling the shows' order so that
different meanings are produced (Joe burns the agent and gets a

girlfriend) and piecing together all they can learn of human society via Joe's diatribes (Joe is an unpaid whore; Joe is made of moldable jelly; human food tastes better when thrown; humans say what is convenient rather than what is true; humans stop and start jerkily like chickens). One bear called 'Angry One' (a respectful Cree term for 'bear') insists on viewing the show between the same two bars every time so that he may see 'every tear on the man's ugly mugg,' while 'Owner of the Earth' lopes back and forth so that the bars blur and he feels a part of the scene. Two of the bears like to re-enact Joe's appearances, yowling and sitting down with heads hung low. Only one bear, Golden Friend, understands that the story is incomplete, showing us only Joe's retrieval of his life, such as it is, but not the scene when it was taken from him, nor the later life-wrecking effects of the time and effectiveness lost, the entropy proceeding from undeserved suffering. 'Honey Paw,' he says, cornering a colleague near the feed door, 'I believe this business with Joe is chaos.'

Honey Paw is so startled by the statement that he does not immediately plunge his snout into the pile of fish delivered through the trapdoor.

Lint is known to have had a memory in which the doctor who presided at his birth was actually some sort of polar bear. Did he regard bears as overmind puppeteers, clinical observers? A fertile area for theory is the fact that there are eleven bears: the bare eleven being two figure ones, implying that both main characters are similar pillars of salt? Or a hint that the story's reasoning is so garbled it would read the same if it were turned upside down? Or are they the eleven faithful apostles, the agent a Judas, and Mary ... Mary?

Another hook (pointed out by the chubby Kip Thorne in *20 Concerns Zine*) is that the agent may represent Lint's concept of 'effortless incitement'—his own real life ability to enrage people to near-apoplexy with little or no effort (or indeed movement). But could

Lint really be attributing this joyous trickster gift to the agent character, when one considers that the story expresses his own rage against his inactive agent? I could say that Lint had had the tables turned on him, were it not for the fact that Lint's agent, Robert Baines, was in fact dead at the time of 'Associate' his desiccated cadaver remaining undetected for decades.

And indeed the true horror of the story is the final glimpse which suggests that the agent may have been human all along—and thus more of a monster than we suspected.

References:
Jeff Lint: A Collection—Jeff Lint (C. Phair Books Inc, 1973)
'Notions Eleven: Interactivity in Lint's 'The Crystalline Associate'—Kip Thorne (*20 Concerns Zine* Issue 3, 1981)
'No-Show at the Joe Show: Why Such Inadequate Security Measures at the Zoo in Lint's 'The Crystalline Associate?'—Jim Smith (*Blast of Merit* zine, 1985)
'Arse Collection and Lint Death Clues'—Reuben Wu (MIT, 1982)

The Lintian Waiter
in 'Tectonic'

Chris Diana

ORIGINALLY PUBLISHED IN 1951, 'Tectonic' is one of Jeff Lint's many 'waiter' stories. It's a queasy tale which seeds the themes which would come to dominate Lint's stories, such as power manipulations, ascended disregard, and audacious tricksterism from the midst of powerlessness. But this tale is different in that, rather than taking the view of the neglected-unto-delirium customers, his protagonist is a waiter, by all appearances suffering from acute doubts during the delivery of a meal. He believes that the entire meal is a sham, constructed with the sole purpose of impeding his understanding of his true duties in life. Most of the beans, for instance, are apparently nothing more than bits of felt, insultingly one-dimensional. Some of them, however, perhaps are real, nominally those responsible for the flavor. The customers appear to be following his movements closely, and sometimes seem about to call out in a bid to affect his behavior. This urge seems to be barely contained.

The meal was ordered three hours ago, when he and the chef were discussing football. Our character got an itch to go upstairs in the restaurant and sleep for an hour. He awoke and saw the chef looking at him with an indeterminate expression on his face. Immediately the memory comes back to him of the meal that had been ordered, and he senses himself to be different from the customers, talking about things they did not understand and barely taking an interest in their concerns. He remembers his suspicions with respect to the menu, which seems to change every few weeks or so. To his way of thinking, this seems designed to confuse him.

Behind the restaurant, he uses a back alley where he can be alone with his thoughts. But every time these thoughts turn towards the menu, trying to discern the patterns, to find the flaws, find out what was behind such a complex operation, something happens that seems to have been created expressly to break his concentration. Sometimes the assistant chef emerges with a tray of leftovers, at other times the chef comes to see how he is doing, or else it is a tearful customer who shows up to question him.

In spite of this, he has a few hours each day for introspection and occupies that time trying to discover the truth. For that, he relies only on his reason and on the evidence of his five senses. Standing in the alley, in the kitchen or in front of a staring customer, the waiter retraces the process of menu, ordering, food preparation and delivery, but in reverse. While the customer arrives at the only certainty that one can have—to wit: 'This waiter is deliberately ignoring me and insulting me at every chance'—Lint's waiter takes that certainty as a point of reference: 'I am a waiter. But must I bring food to customers?'

At this point in the story, the initial impression of the reader, that the waiter is an insane moron, hardens. Yet the waiter's perception of the futility of his routine are so accurate and verifiable, that his motivations are by no means alien. Suspended in our uncertainty with respect to the interpretation of the story, we are fully prepared for the ending: our hero lays down on a table at which three diners are seated, and on falling asleep, receives the blessings due those who have triangulated upon the perfect social affront for the occasion: one which turns a lock. At two in the morning, the shock of abrupt awakening and the chef's spluttering, incandescent rage make him understand that he has crossed the line from pettily imposed duty into fuller selfhood. The chef leaves the restaurant, encounters the assistant chef behind a dumpster and, finally, we discover that they are not even human, but tailors who take human form to deceive the waiter and customers and thus prevent themselves from being recognized and shamed. Many of the meals we have witnessed are instantly explained.

The hero of 'Tectonic' therefore, is right: he should delay or entirely avoid serving the guests. But why does he alone suspect that all is not as it seems?

Lint does not answer this directly, but gives a few good hints. In the first place, the bearing of the average waiter suggests that he is someone very important—the center of the universe, in fact. The waiter may also be an extremely powerful person—diners fear what may happen if he were to become offended. Finally, the average waiter believes himself to have no need for bodily sustenance. I myself have heard one to claim while bringing soup: 'I transcend this petty feasting; its span of hours is but a casual phase in my experience. Second only to the prime datum of my own existence is the certainty of my own pounding continuity. I have neither beginning nor end.' During his sleep, Lint's waiter becomes that which he is; he experiences a profound and relieving sensation of being united with one facet of his satisfaction. 'Sleep! Sleep everywhere! It was good to be with his own comfort—good to recall even dimly that everyone was aware of him, confounded by him, exasperated, enraged and baffled as he denied them.'

Faced with all that, the conclusion at which we arrive about the identity of this mysterious character becomes practically irrefutable. It is nothing less than Fatty Arbuckle himself.

And Your Point Is?

Not, however, the Arbuckle traditionally imagined by occidental religions—a transcendent being isolated from its creation, hovering above reality and governing the world from an exalted position. Lint's waiter is the Arbuckle identified with nature, which only exists to the measure in which someone is imagining him as being so. (Jack Marsden in Lint's *The Caterer* also praises the Buddha-like comedian.)

From this point of view, the tailor/chefs are creatures who decline to aspire to an independent, individual existence and prefer some kind of anonymous absorption in social function. Speaking rigorously, that is impossible in terms of this story, since all of the customers are so painfully conscious of their reliance upon them that they have attained the status of angry deities to whom the patient diners offer up prayers. They also cannot feel empathy with the chefs, because they do not understand the reasons (if such exist) for the delay. 'Perhaps,' they think, 'the chefs are not there.'

When the waiter recovers his true self-respect, the diners recover their ability to express full-blown outrage. If not a major Lint story, 'Tectonic' is an unrelenting one. At a length of only 1,108 words, it packs the emotional punch of a buzzard hitting a windscreen.

Stress & Spillover
in Three Lint Plays

Steve Aylett

IT SEEMS THAT, in his foray into playwriting in the late 1960s, Lint gave up on any hope at being understood and this abandon was quite freeing for him, apparently forming the basis of his philosophy of *carnagio*, 'the energy of collapse too long resisted.' As Dennis Ofstein has stated, Lint created plays which were unsettling only to those who are unaware enough to be 'settled' in the midst of the world's nightmare and, in the case of something like *The Riding On Luggage Show*, 'salted the soil so densely that anyone purporting to do anything interesting in the future had to pretend that *Luggage* had never happened.' Below are brief descriptions of three Lint plays.

27 Workshy Slobs

27 WORKSHY SLOBS was written to portray how a town's entire tempo changes when a dog is elected mayor. The setting of the play is Krilltown and the structure is broken up into three basic 'dirges' that together render the play useless. Act I opens with the election of an uncomprehending dog to Mayor accompanied with all the rosy-cheeked hope and celebratory hat throwing that attends large-scale social error. Act II changes to a dazed, awkward realization of what has occurred, and Act III finishes with a sort of frenzy of avoidance and damage, as if men might blur themselves into non-accountability. Time jumps by several days in the play, and the audience is also left feeling that they have spent several days watching the unfolding of these dismal events. It is not unheard of for audience members to climb up on stage and punch characters to the floor. That Lint suspected as much is hinted in his direction that the actors 'not be surprised at anything, no matter where it comes from, especially near the end of the interminable second act.' His intentions do not become completely apparent until the funeral scene in Act III, when the dog bursts out of the coffin alive and runs amok among the audience with a saddle of dynamite strapped to its back. Life then is revealed to the audience from beyond the grave and gives it a new perspective that is both understandable and regrettable.

The characters are simple and uncomplicated, centering on the Stern and the Cane families who are enemies in Krilltown. The play, more particularly, focuses on Libby Stern and Brad Cane whose relationship gives the play its one and only point of interest for the individual. The characters, as a whole, are not very intelligent, but do portray what life truly is about in a small town that elects a spaniel for Mayor. We can all admire that.

Lint called *Slobs* his 'normal play.' There are no giant whale-heads thrust up through stage floor around which the actors must shuffle with barely any room (*Born With a Double Skull*) nor are massive cannons fired at the audience (*The Ravaged Face of Saggy Einstein*) nor swarms of locusts released (*I Love You*). Lint said 'it will show people that this is the way I could have written if I had less energy, and fewer ideas of my own. This is the way the theatre will die, very soon I think.' But it still outshines most other plays for curt dialogue and unexpected eruptions of tear-rashed hysteria, as almost every character realizes what a mockery they have just made of civilization.

Libby Stern, one of the most lethargic characters in the play, is used by Lint to show the relative wisdom of avoiding the crowd, as you are therefore likely to dodge the commission of evil and bullshit more or less by default. Libby is a character who is normal enough that the audience could relate to her and yet intelligent in little ways that take people by surprise. Without going through normal emotions the character would seem alien to the audience; yet she is uninterested in the Mayoral election and, hearing of the result, merely draws a simple picture of a dog, which is later projected against the back of the stage during the dynamite dog rampage. When Libby says that all she expects of a dog is that it try to be happy, many of us can agree. Lint included the scene because he believed that even though there is a basic idea of a dog's function in society, its true function is to suit itself. If the dog didn't have any likes and dislikes, it would be faceless; what we believe to be the mere architectural features of a dog are in fact a true expression of emotion. Lint's stage dog is portrayed uniquely in its own way and is full of beans.

Brad Cane represents a wise yet ratlike man in a world of eager fellas. Brad is not unreasonable in his requirement that all address him as 'my liege.' He is one of the few people in town who understands the meaning of the term. He is able to defend his face from the many blows of the Meeting Leader's hammer while still giving a speech in support of equal rights. It is necessary for a man with a high and ideal view of justice to defend his face, even if he does so hopelessly. He is wise enough to know that the moose which sticks its head into the town hall meeting room briefly, then withdraws, is a message from the universe.

This effect is rarely impressive on stage, as the front of a stuffed moose is merely rolled into view and then drawn back. Often a horse, cow or large hen is used, and the animal is withdrawn again too quickly to register with most audience members. Jesse Curry has opined that by this time most of the audience are too mentally fried anyway to register or be surprised by anything. In any case, Brad denies that the moose was ever there. When the assembly breaks up, he warns the townspeople that they cannot leave through the outer hallway because it is choc-a-block with 'henry eels.' Mary Thyme, the local gossip, snorts her scorn and opens the door to release a flood of eels onto the stage, many of which inevitably flop and thrash onto the front row of the audience, Brad laughing the while. (Brad was played by Bruce Dern in its first Consolation Playhouse production.) According to Lint's specifications each eel should be fitted with small rubber horns, this being his idea of what a 'henry eel' should look like. Few audience members comply with these instructions, however, despite their repeatedly being stated over the house PA from the moment the eels appear.

Brad teaches people that they must learn to be frequently attacked and tormented, either by he himself or someone else with a different point of view. He is an outstanding challenge to both the grim and the blithe. He alone laughs during the eel eruption; he alone laughs during the dynamite dog rampage—in fact, Lint writes, 'he is flushed and bent over, having laughed away all his air.' At the absolute apex of the chaos and of his hilarity, the Meeting Leader turns and levels all the blame at Cane in gigantically declamatory terms. Everything grows silent as a spotlight irises in upon Cane, who seems to have become a small monkey with an 'incredibly small face barely bigger than a raisin.' The monkey fidgets a bit in place, looking about him in the silence, and the spotlight winks closed into darkness. Darkness remains until it dawns upon the appalled, abused audience that the play has ended and that the venue doors might now be found to be unlocked. From beginning to end their needs have not been mentioned or catered for.

When questioned, Lint wouldn't admit to knowing what an audience was. Lint kept his self-respect.

Slave Labor For Lovers

RARELY IN LITERATURE are characters presented as victims of sheep, but when it happens it's a sight for sore eyes. There are several examples of this in Jeff Lint's controversial play, *Slave Labor For Lovers*. The play caused a lot of pretend-debate regarding the roles of humans and animals in society. Some of the audience members noticed similarities between themselves and the characters that were presented as sheep victims, because the cast would watch the theatregoers as they entered and then quickly dressed up to 'impersonate' them on stage. The treatment meted out to these doppelgangers was shocking and disturbing.

Leonard Bayard is a typical fifties-era husband, with a wife, three children, a dog and a well paid job. Bayard becomes a victim of a sheep which batters its way in through a set of French doors and bites him in the crotch. As Lorrie Rice has observed, 'It's quite evident that Bayard is unhappy and uncomfortable with the idea. Bayard had everything he could possibly want in life. This is the major reason why Bayard does not want to be attacked by a sheep, in case it affects his image and gives him a bad reputation. Bayard would do anything to stop having to be attacked like that, ever again.' This is evident in the scene when Bayard tries to cover up the sheep's body with some turf. 'I must try to bury it somehow. This thing must be hushed up at any price.'

After killing the sheep with a spade, Bayard tries his best to live up to every expectation society sets for him. The idea of maintaining a strong image in the community is of bewildering importance to Bayard. He tells his neighbor, who witnessed him whacking the sheep over the head, 'you will not find me lacking in cash for you and your family if you only keep quiet about that little scene.'

And Your Point Is?

In Act 2, we are able to see how the affects of the sheep attack have taken a toll on Bayard's thinking. 'Sheep work in the opposite way to danger, don't they, normally?' he wonders aloud, and worries constantly that his wife is aware of the incident. Bayard resolves to act the hero, claiming to one and all that sheep have become a threat, and goes out with a shotgun. 'Often I have wished some terrible danger might threaten you all,' he tells everyone at a town meeting, 'So I could offer my life and blood, everything, for your sake. Thanks be to heaven, you are threatened now. Kill, kill, kill!'

Bayard feels his only out is to attempt to massacre an entire field full of sheep, which become enraged and stampede into the village. The mayor is knocked down and three sheep chew on his 'hams.' The sheriff is knocked through the front window of a store. A sheep springs up at an old lady's face and bites her nose, after which she swings around and around, the sheep finally letting go and flying against an electricity generator. During these scenes Frank Sinatra's 'It Was a Very Good Year' is played over the speakers. For the audience members being impersonated on stage, the combination of this song and the violence done to their image created a traumatic experience. Added to this was the fact that, in the tradition of Lint's 'carnagio' plays, many real animals were mixed in among the stuffed and costumed ones and these were furtively encouraged to leave the stage and cavort among the audience.

In Act 3, Bayard feels such remorse that he surrenders to the sheep's ideas and expectations, laying down in a field and allowing them physical control over him. Arms spread wide in crucifixion, he is carried upon a sea of sheep's backs as the *Hallelujah Chorus* plays. Seeing this crowdsurfing apparition, his wife decides that she no longer needs Leonard in her life. She tells the police chief in hospital, 'When I saw him glide and sway on that sea of wool, my blood ran cold,' showing that she is more interested in worn-out metaphors than expressing original ideas. When the police chief responds by saying

'Leave me alone! I can't live like this!' we know how he feels. In the sheep's eyes, Bayard is now merely a possession who, like a toy, can be played with and cast aside.

It's not only obvious Leonard Bayard is pathetically reliant on lambs, but it's now evident that his marriage and business (Bayard Foreign Marketing) had been a fabrication for the sake of appearances. Not only is his wife a victim of the herd, but of Leonard as well. It is surprising that Lint allowed someone like her to clutter up the stage.

A Team Becomes Embers Together
'I DON'T FEEL much of anything. Not with this horse on top of me.' That, said by Billy Imes in Lint's musical *The Riding On Luggage Show*, was definitely a sentiment Tony Shardik could have expressed in the beautifully baffling rock opera *A Team Becomes Embers Together*. Too many winters in Marjoram Town have taken its toll on Tony Shardik, and he is so sleepy he doesn't really wake up anymore. Shardik never gets to finish his explanations about anything and falls forward into his meals from time to time. 'I Lack Stamina,' he sings, lounging around. Shardik is irritated that he has to stand up every day to pop a snail from his window. Realizing it must be the same snail each time, he takes it out of town and throws it into some snow. The moment the snail leaves town every minute of Shardik's life becomes better. He shouts at the sky: 'The disguised cannot see me!' He becomes nature's antagonist, the one who ends up killing many innocent snails who were only defending their country.

Lint complicates the story in that Shardik becomes flawed morally to such an extent that the outside forces of light and gravity are deflected from his forehead in a blast of 'heavy energy.' Shardik claims to a frazzled nun that almost all of his motions create this by-product, a dark oil only he can perceive, and which weighs upon him. 'Nobody is clean,' she assures him, then runs cackling in a circle as green smoke blasts upward—she disappears like the Wicked Witch of the West.

'What the hell do you mean, nobody's clean?' Shardik yells down at the trapdoor through which she descended. 'What the hell are you?' He tries prizing the trapdoor open but collapses, defeated. The nun appears behind him. 'Exactly what's the matter? What's the matter? What's the matter? What's the matter?' She keeps asking it over and over of the startled Shardik, who scrabbles backward as she advances, her demand growing louder and more caustic every second. Eleven human skeletons flop down from the rafters, jangling and clattering on strings as Shardik pushes them aside and stumbles to escape. Here the song 'You Lack Stamina' bursts out, apparently sung by the skeletons, which seem to attempt a formation dance but are too tangled, battered and floaty to give it any coherence. (Lint states that it should be 'a tapdance during which the skeletons rarely touch the ground.') At the song's conclusion the skeletons' skulls burst by means of squibs—these detonations are not spectacular, sounding no louder than a cap gun, and often audience members fail to notice them. One must wonder what kind of morals such people have.

'I'm not afraid,' Shardik cries, as the skeletons float upward out of sight. 'I know who I am and the extent of my energies.' If, as Shardik says, he has lied to nobody, it is the community of Marjoram that cannot handle the consequences. Shardik has become a man, something that never interested him. He starts apologizing to every snail he can find, until a snail the size of a Volkswagon glides onto the stage and starts to sing 'No Stamina,' its antlers moving slowly. It seems perfectly friendly, though, and glides off again as the song concludes.

Audiences should not be deceived, however. Soon after the snail leaves the stage, Jofy enters with the empty shell of the animal and claims that she caught a midget capering with it near the old sheds. This implied double meaning of the word 'shed' is probably as close as the play comes to having a point.

The nun re-enters dragging the skeletons negligently in one tangled bundle, and leaves them with Shardik, saying he can 'Do what you want' with them. Shardik stands staring at the useless mess in total unmoving silence for exactly seven minutes, before exploding suddenly into a crazy, hectic, flailing dance as he sings 'Loss of Stamina.' Spotlights are swooping around the theatre and glitter and confetti rains down upon the audience, who are by this time boiling over with furious exasperation at having almost two hours of their time wasted on this load of balls. A huge American flag drops down to form the stage backdrop as Shardik finishes the song at the top of his lungs, down on one knee, arms wide, and the entire stage catches fire around him. As smoke fills the theatre and Shardik remains absolutely immobile with arms akimbo (Lint suggests that after five minutes he should be furtively replaced with a flammable dummy bearing a drooling wax face), the doors are unlocked and the audience is allowed to stream coughing and stunned into the street. It has been reported that on three separate occasions patrons sustained serious injury after stumbling into the path of oncoming traffic. Thus for the lucky few their indignation was quickly forgotten.

A superstition has arisen in theatreland that it is unlucky to mention *A Team Becomes Embers Together* by name, and so it is alluded to merely as 'the stupid play.' It is made absolutely clear to its audience that the cast are to be sympathized with rather than cursed, yet the ill-fortune of the play's performers seems derived from the perfectly understandable feelings of an audience trapped and abused when expecting entertainment. Most exit the experience feeling troubled at best, and at worst, full of vengeful fury. This is the source of the many chokings and falls down stairs sustained by its actors, up to and including the very public and verifiable occasion in 1970 of Shardik being strangled by a stage-invader during his seven minutes silence. What impresses more than Lint's ability to incite such passion is that it all seems effortless.

'Deep Vanishing' in Jeff Lint's Science Fiction*

Alfred Bork

IN THIS PAPER I will show how Jeff Lint aided the long-delayed departure of science fiction from its ambivalent position in literary circles and pop culture. Once being written as mere 'escapism,' 'entertainment' and 'shit,' after the fifties the popular SF genre gained a different tincture. By the novels of Lint we became aware of narrative devices and techniques of the SF genre which were formerly disguised to save our embarrassment. Their one-dimensionality thus gave way to the constant effrontery, resentment and playfulness in the works of Lint.

Jeff Lint, one of the most original and derided post-war science fiction writers of America, constructed and celebrated a world of fiction in which there is a constant but easy swerving aside from the pre-accepted 'nobhead' dialectics of the traditional science fiction genre. That genre is usually accepted as popular fiction because of its huge book industry, prolific writers and over-reliance on space fairies. However, it has its literary geniuses as well, like Jeff Lint, whom William R. Strong calls 'the Christopher Walken of science fiction.'[1]

And Your Point Is?

One of the reasons why Lint's earliest stories in particular appeal to screenwriters is their richness in metaphors which lend themselves to lazy interpretations and crap elaborations, so that a script can be based on Lint but have no resemblance to anything Lint would have tolerated were he not completely rotted down.

The popular topology of SF includes the exotic and the alien ('Aliens invade—and they're delicious!'). Inevitably the great number of books written in this goofy genre falls into the category of consumer-friendly fiction; consumer-friendly as they give easy pleasure to the reader but nothing more than a few stinking dollars to the authors. This stigma sticks more with SF than any other genre—including the billion-dollar market in specialist so-called 'tentacle' fiction.[2] Yet when we read a Jeff Lint novel, at first we see the globular and throbbing world of a SF writer, but as we go on we see sniggering stag beetles, frozen eels used for furniture, and other trash of this variety, so that the linear pace of the story becomes like a fond (if exaggerated) memory from childhood. This is the diabolic nature of touching an alien ideology just with the tip of your tongue to get a flavor, only to find your nose (and lips) on fire.

Lint begins his novels having an idea inside of his head and a lack of interest in the normal values of interpersonal relationships in a standard narrative. Somewhere in the process of writing and thinking reciprocally he may remember the uninteresting way that the average person is supposed to behave and is thus reassured that he must stick to what he planned before. Implications of this phenomenon can be traced in the minds of his characters and in their almost complete lack of interest in anything standard-issue. In his own words, Lint tells us the gist of his writing: 'It's not difficult to be funnier than god, is it? Genuine creativity will, by definition, result in something new and never seen before. But despite people's claims that they welcome or crave originality, their dislike of the new and unfamiliar means that any encounter with real creativity will always send them scampering away—perhaps giggling nervously like tarts, at best.' [3]

Keep in mind that he wrote his major works not only in the 1960s and 1970s, but in the vacuum of the 1980s, a period considered (at least prior to the early 2000s) to be the culmination of man's wish to function without thought, imagination or indeed anything of interest. Thus it is quite impressive to find that that decade's sterility had no diminishing effect on his work. In fact, Lint once theorized on 'beading,' the gathering of generally unwanted imaginative energy to nodal points during times of social conservatism: he himself being one of those nodal points. This was probably a bit of bullshit invented on the spot, as Lint seems always to have worked entirely independently of the prevailing social color levels. More than anything the mood of dismissive individuality that billows like unexpected steam out of his novels is the most significant contemporary sensibility with which he supplemented the SF genre.

Science fiction is a genre that makes use of the political, the historic and the social to garb space gnomes in a cloak of glamor that they are unlikely to have selected in actuality. This standard-issue content is a result of its barely-examined acceptance of progress in technological, ideological, economic, religious and social life. In this respect postmodern fiction and science fiction intersect. As a result we can say that the postmodern awareness of the political, the idealized and the historical are quite at home in the realm of fantasy.

One more significant characteristic both science fiction and post-modern fiction share is the uninteresting 'lardy'[4] handling of their subject matter. For example, technology and the materializing of everyday life is put under shallow, unimaginative suspicion in Asimov's novels. Many science fiction writers fall short of foregrounding the ontological questions that their texts pose, except some writers like Lint, who incessantly mystifies and irritates the reader in the process of reading, by introducing new concepts such as 'jack lenses' and barn elves in the very last sentence of his stories. He uses the speculative realm of this genre to explore the nature of stupidity and its never-ending ignorance of itself. Thus, it is hard to find a writer as annoying as Jeff Lint in the general SF corpus. Lint shows us the complete lack of paradox in modern life which is evident if we look at it honestly and with an acceptance of its detail.

As Jeff Lint rendered more than eleven conclusions upon as many subjects in his novels, to summate his career with a single conclusion is impossible. Nevertheless, if I am to hold a position as far as Lint's work is concerned, I know with clarity that he is one of the most obstinately original and therefore most un-American writers, whose relation to either the SF genre or the 'vortexan'[5] genre cannot be pinpointed with ease. Martin Orteca says in his essay on the 'trembly' place of Lint among his rivals, that he deals with the effective illegality of honesty and he uses different strategies than the SF writers that came before and after him, thus perhaps being one who 'broke with the continuity of literature's development' — and thus, like all those ahead of their time, will be simply left out of that continuity in the official records.[6] That is why I find both naively charming and horrifying the constant emphasis on postmodern subjectivity in our modern world, while those authorities who encourage and profit by that trend in the populace privately covet the hard facts.

As I said before, with his style Lint challenged the dullness of a human batch limited by fashion to a cycle of repeated patterns separated by excitable/feeble forgetfulness. Human motivation alters in novels like *Turn Me Into a Parrot* in which we can find neither stereotypes nor type A-Z meat puppets of the psychological tradition. Through my analysis, one thing especially attracted my tired eyes. The novels *Slogan Love, Dragons of Aggrazar, Doomed and Confident*, and all three Arkwitch books, share the concept of 'soul-saving resentments.' As a writer and an original human Lint was overtly sensitive to the culminations in personality manufacture inherent in mass science, society, religion, politics and cultural phenomena. He suggested that none of these were desirable sources of belief. Never does he preach contrarianism, except for the least promising beginner. Effronteries, which are always lustily enjoyed in Lint, create a colorful medium which is the mere anteroom to a larger realm of fully considered individuality.

Furthermore, I have found various vortical topics with which Lint was concerned, such as entropy, lethargy, forgery, snails, historicity, authorship, the berserk blame reflex, mud, bursts of sarcasm from 'etherically adjacent' realms, etc., all of which are embroidered into off-the-peg tropes of classical SF such as robots, computer simulation, sea monkeys, alternate and even less interesting futures, exotic spacedrives, organ sentience, and more.

As Kip Thorne noted: 'He wasn't too interested in the standard genre furniture for its own sake. When he had to mention it as a mere plot point he was sometimes quite slapdash, as in his description of an astronaut who remained in suspended animation "for ages." He always wanted to get to the main point, then a thousand more main points immediately after. Why waste time?'[7]

It is difficult to do an analytical study of Lint's novels, as the virtue of his texts lie in their 'Lintalia,' the details which excite an emotion which has no name. I can say that in Lint we find a pointillist universe of joyous disregard for culturally imposed uncertainties/long-term manipulation systems, an author who looks honestly at the 24/7 cruelties of humanity. In addition to all these interpretations, the taboo position of honestly admitted powerlessness blasts a purifying light through Lint's novels (perhaps most evidently in *Clowns and Locusts*). In *The Stupid Conversation*, *Fanatique* and *The Phosphorous Tarot of Matchbooks* his protagonist is therefore able to move forward with all chaff discarded and an accurate view of the circumstances to be dealt with. Lint's starting point is a place that less honest/imaginative authors never reach. However, we realize that Arkwitch is not a hero in the standard, false sense. A joy exists in the sheer mischief of seeing clearly and having the blithe gall to speak of it amid the stinking swamp of humanity's evasions.

[1] 'Jeff Lint: dead and not shy about expressing it'—William R. Strong (*Good People Quarterly*, 1998)

[2] for early examples of this phenomenon see *Here's That Sick Squid I Owe You* (collected stories from *Maximum Tentacles Magazine*) (Phair Press, 1974)

[3] Interview, *Montauk Magazine*, 1970

[4] see 'No Argument Here' by Charles Thomas Sell (*Shrimp Song Journal*, 1988) in which he agrees (with nobody, apparently) that people's fat cells have a precocious intelligence of their own.

[5] see *Reader, I Dissolved Him*, Chris Gaynor's history of the Vortexan movement and Taylor Gimli's supposed 'spunk rampage' (Dern, 1996)

[6] see 'Hinton? I Don't Know Any Hinton' by Cynthia Bora (*Science Journal of New England*, Vol XXI issue 5)

[7] 'Dodecahedron of Love: Floods of Tears and the "Final Girl" in Jeff Lint's "The Last True Page"'—Kip Thorne (*20 Concerns Zine*, Issue 5, 1982)

See also:

'Jeff Lint: Don't Be Light'—Martin Orteca (*Kitten Time Zine*, 2002)

Jeff Lint: A Collection—Jeff Lint (Phair Press, 1973)

'The Lint Resentment Power Grid' (uncredited diagram) (*J-Lint Zine*, 1992)

* Jeff Lint spoke of (and demonstrated) two kinds of vanishing: shallow vanishing, in which he seemed to step around a corner in the air and disappear into empty space; and deep vanishing, in which he simply walked away.

'Rise of the Swans':
Doing Bird With Jeff Lint

Steve Aylett

JEFF LINT'S SOFTLY apocalyptic story 'Dawn of the Swans' first appeared in a 1958 issue of speciality pulp mag *Giant Feather* and was later collected in the book *Mask of Disapproval* (as 'Rise of the Swans'). In this unsettling yarn a thick, wet fog rises from the great park lake at the centre of the city in which the narrator lives, enveloping the city for three days. All electronic devices are damped out and occasional screams and bursts of sarcasm are heard from the smog. When the marsh mists finally disperse the narrator finds that the city has been overtaken by sentient swans. Our hero is Mario Drake, a survivalist type who, suspecting some government chemical experiment of the Winnipeg variety, has used the three days to arm himself to the teeth and is dismayed to find the city towers merely ticked with swans like white pterodactyls.

After a disillusioning patch during which he tries to organize his fellow humans into a revolutionary unit, he finds that they are just as boring and nerveless as before the Dawn. Meanwhile the swans are not lording it over the humans, and actually seem quite organized and honest. The story really kicks off when Drake has an audience with Quine, the King Swan, though this includes an absolutely mind-bending debate on the nature of time:

'A clock is a cage placed in a flowing stream; holding nothing, stopping nothing, not even for a minute.'

'A man's smiles don't queue up—they all happen the same place. Time is what separates them.'

'The same conclusion directed backwards can be used as an excuse. One season does not outwit another.'

'Only the forgetful grant clemency to the past.'

Assembled onlookers are barking, honking and hissing throughout the exchange, but only the swans are laughing. By the time Quine has told Drake 'Even a rose shoulders space for itself,' Drake is suffering a delirium in which he believes the black knob on the top of Quine's bill is a tiny melted Bible, a misperception Quine begins to correct before realizing he himself doesn't know what the hell it is.

Drake organizes a system of water channels to run alongside the city sidewalks and is soon an honorary general with white chevrons on his shoulders, much to the disgust of the black swan general Castalan. Indulging in revelry among these bleached pteranodons who are now reorganizing human affairs everywhere, Drake learns their weird and graceful world-view and suffers intense origami dreams in which angles are bent so far the wrong way they end up right. He falls in love with a girl swan called Ymel, mesmerized by her puffy white cheeks which he names 'Bosun' and 'Freddy Armitage' (though they never respond). He is also happy with the marriage because swans are known to be monogamous. A child results, a human girl with the wings of a swan: the first true angel.

So much for the basic story.[1] However, it's thrown off-beam by a misprint which appeared at first publication in *Giant Feather* magazine, and which was carried over into the *Disapproval* collection:

Drake's parents are said to have died when he was young, after which he was 'raised by two ants.' This unconventional upbringing throws unintended motivational vertices over Drake's behavior in the story, suggesting an unusual psychology in the hero. Lint, however, had written Drake as an average sort of man. Later in the story, a proof-reader must have actively changed 'aunts' to 'ants' to make it consistent with the term's earlier appearance, so that Drake sits on a stone sky balcony musing, 'If only those crazy ants of mine could see this.' Thus he was not only raised by ants, but 'crazy' ants. The ant error totally undermines the philosophical thrust of Lint's story, making it difficult for many readers to identify with Drake or to trust his observations. Some critics (eg. Cameo Herzog in the article 'If I Could but Kill') have suggested that Lint deliberately included the notion that Drake had been raised by ants, then had later thought it was a crappy idea and blamed it on the sub-editors.

Edward A. Clark has proposed that the entire business with the swans is being imagined in Drake's thick head. (Cameo Herzog writes with the casual certainty that Drake is dreaming it all up 'in the bath.')[2] Drake gains in status by these imaginings, especially when one considers that the status is not bestowed by human beings. If it is a dream, are there clues to Drake's real circumstances hidden in the dream? There are several references to glass, lenses and spectacles (the scholarly swan Lupar wears wireframed specs). Is Drake an optometrist, or is this a nod to altered perceptions; or both? In my opinion Lint would not resort to such a cliché unless it was to cloak a more interesting possibility—that the swan empire has long existed and that human beings are considered creatures of lurid myth and science fiction. Subtle clues to this can be seen in the bacchanalia scene, where it is claimed that Drake scrutinizes things with his 'third eye,' that he has a 'hollow leg,' and that his fully engorged cock reaches a mere 'seven inches.' This chimera makes it clear that we have gone from a human empire, to swan/human coexistence, to a swan empire without the existence of humanity, the deeper we have explored the story's subtext. Lint's own ambiguity about the human race is crystallized in a less comical and more affecting chimera—that of the human/swan/ angel creature. Did a part of Lint want humanity ('the maker and eater of lies') to exist in some form after all?

When asked in an interview with Daniel Guyal whether Drake is hallucinating the swan uprising, Lint replied gloomily 'We'll probably never know.' Then he perked up and added: 'But seriously, no. No, he isn't.' (Guyal reports that Lint then began making a strange 'keening' noise while leaning forward and staring at him with gluey eyes of need.) This does not eliminate the possibility that the swans are hallucinating the man.[3]

Lint scholars have rampaged over the Drake/Quine debate. Believing that he argues for his race, Drake tells Quine that laws and systems are 'not personal.'

Quine replies: 'Everything's personal, Drake. Everything that happens to a person.'

The second half of the story includes a tribunal presided over by a strange, furless and palpitant badger. In fact this creature is so cute that no-one in the courtroom can concentrate enough to be efficient, serious or bad-tempered. The whole thing becomes vague and oddly hysterical. Peculiarly accommodating remarks gum up the proceedings. The camera's eye of the story seems to hove in on Drake as he melts into a slow-bloom happiness with the new state of affairs in his nation. The swan empire seems to be stupid and harmless, rather than stupid and malicious. Indeed the cygnutopia of 'Dawn' is a rare example of Lint looking amiably upon a social set-up, all the more unusual for his aliens' tendency not to bother landing on Earth, and his spacemen's rather jaded view of alien cultures ('Aluminum flagstones? What's the point?') And it seems to have fallen together. At story's end Drake and his family look into the night sky. 'Stars are accidents. How many?'

As Alfred Bork has said, 'Lint shows us the complete lack of paradox in modern life which is evident if we look at it honestly and with an acceptance of its detail.'

Lint took the arterial route to people's honesty in books as chemically complex as diamondback venom, a gasping refreshment next to the works of Asimov, Amis, DeLillo and other literary flatearthers. 'Turn the day about with these cold star swine?' he wrote. 'I do not need to be alone for my smile or frown to be in my own hands.' His characters spoke words from what he called 'the other side of the face,' something we could use in an age when any long thought with the temerity to emerge is cut up like a worm, action is like lighting a match on a mirror and truth is regarded as the worst version.

In bringing on the swans, Lint retakes that old world in which actual progress was maybe possible. Man and the swan seem in agreement on attempting to make life a bit more bearable rather than fussing about whether humanity represents the pinnacle of creation: this issue can be sorted out later if, by some 'bizarre yet boring' twist, the matter becomes important. (That notion of 'bizarre yet boring' recurs in Lint as the telltale quality of human affairs; its drab flag and flavor.) Bork has observed that 'the taboo position of honestly admitted powerlessness blasts a purifying light through Lint's novels.' This allows Lint's protagonists to start a tale with an accurate view of the circumstances to be confronted (a point which other authors' protagonists rarely reach by the end). Critics have complained that Lint's stories lack conflict—they do, in fact, conflict with every story written by everyone else.

Footnotes

[1] Some of which ended up in Chris Caccamise's crappy but successful novel-length plagiarism, *Empire of Flamingos* (not to mention the appalling British feature-length cartoon *Attack of the Piglets*, voiced

entirely by Bernard Cribbins).

[2] Lint friend and fellow pulp author Marshall Hurk wrote a variation on the 'locked room' mystery, in which Cameo Herzog seems to come up with an idea, in a bare, locked, soundproofed room. All means of communication are tested, all possibilities eliminated, and yet Herzog has thought of one more idea than he had when he entered the room. The trick, of course, is that this is another man who happens to have that name. Hurk had never described the man's appearance, nor explicitly stated that the prisoner was the critic and journalist Cameo Herzog.

[3] Such hallucinations of brave men feature in Lint's prophetic 'Too Fat to Riot.'

Sources:

Mask of Disapproval—Jeff Lint (Rich & Cowan, 1961)

Giant Feather (Collected Tales)—editor Allen Walsh (Chaffee, 1976)

'If I Could but Kill' by Cameo Herzog (collected in *Dust We Shall Become: Collected Reviews of Cameo Herzog*—Balkan Books, 1969)

'Look Here, Upon This Picture'—Marshall Hurk (*Bewildering Stories* 1959)

'Deep Vanishing in Jeff Lint's Science Fiction'—Alfred Bork (Portland State University, Oregon, 2003)

'Swans, Apes, What's the Fucking Difference?'—Ian Watson (*Jellysump Zine*)

'Swan Lee, Swanley and Swans: the Barrett/Kent/Lint Connection'—Debra Copelan (*J-Lint* fanzine, 1994)

Inconvenience From Outer Space

Michael H. Hersh

INTRODUCTION: Pointedly Ignoring the Overmind

UNTIL 1971, FEWER serious attempts had been made to understand the meaning of science fiction as a genre than had been made to understand the expressions on the faces of cats. Cats, after all, are funny, glossy, and basically just fantastic. The editors and writers of the pulp magazines too often saw science fiction as at best limited and at worst pathetically useless compared to even the least active or personable of these spring-loaded mammals. Hugo Gernsback would weep with despair if he saw one. 'What reason have I to continue,' he wrote in 1932, 'when one look from one of those fluffy babies can render me without purpose.'

But what these practitioners had tended to ignore was the covetous quality of SF. Camus has described how the artist works through selection, by isolating the unique in the context of the universal: 'Chickens, the universe, an eye. All are my chubby friends.'[1] CS Lewis has likened the series of events that occurs within a story to a net designed to catch an elusive something else, and he did this so clumsily and obviously in his own books that the smirking remark about nets was not required from him or anybody.

Recent attempts at defining the genre have tended to crystallize around two perspectives: the flabbily sarcastic, and what may be called the 'stern.' According to the flabby perspective, conventional literature rarely deals with the individual, leaning instead toward bellicose friendships and group relationships; science fiction is angled in its field of concern toward larger (though still boring) groupings. 'It is because of this fundamental orientation of the tentacle-obsessed mind that science fiction, serving readers with a sort of "tentacle training," treats imaginative themes in the ways it does; that it invents crunchy new kinds of spider, for instance; new societies, huge sweeps of jam, that it moves outward and generalizes, that it concentrates on speed-variable machinery and employs sense-dulling cliché.'[2] Again, Brandon Carr has written: 'In freeze-dried fiction, praise is given to a quality in the individual that arises from ignorance of the self—man as a creature of ethical evasion. In SF, the target of appraisal is man as a creature of two arms, two legs, maybe more. The implications for public policy are: Do the properties of civilization serve humans en masse, or bugs en masse, both, neither?'[3]

The 'stern' perspective, on the other hand, concentrates on the way in which SF deliberately deviates from the world-as-experienced in terms of its patently made-up settings. Critics such as Cameo Herzog and Douglas Hurd have stressed how useless this is to one and all, and in so doing have noted SF's relation to older forms of time-wasting (sport, jam-making, sniggering etc). Indeed, Hurd would prefer to abandon the term 'science fiction' in favor of the term 'nothing.'

These two perspectives are not mutually exclusive—quite the contrary. Essentially, they describe 'bones and barley'—as evidenced by Hurd's statement above. In arguing for a definition of SF as 'stories of being briefly entangled in alien species of bracken,'

Michael H. Hersh

Giles T Hatton gives a nod to both perspectives.[4]

As a quill hen, reader, or critic, then, one may view a piece of work on a too-faint-to-see/too-big-to-confront scale. In mimetic fiction the standard-issue spaceman is confronted with an angular context, at which he must stare for punishing amounts of time. Any characteristics which would differentiate him from other human beings and give him a uniqueness would also serve as the source of other humans' problems in integrating him into their society. In science fiction the bendy legs of the hero are subject to changes in gravity, and in this the unique characteristics he lacks are supposed to recede from view, for the focus of attention is intended to be elsewhere (his legs). Problems arise not so much from anything which might differentiate him from his fellows, but from a jumpy spider (present or potential) which he does not share with them—even if, as is often the case, he later unwittingly transports the spider back to earth in his stupid ship.

The writer of science fiction explores that region where mankind ignores the unassimilated outer universe. SF, then, exists as one side of the spectrum of strategies for preserving the human evasion in 'fictional jelly.' Conceived of as tentacle fantasy, it has a dark and miserable heritage. Science fiction is a convulsion of fantasy that outfits itself with the garments of the squid-fighting hero in order to explore the long-answered 'question' of the potential man's absorption into the bland and avoidance of larger and/or more interesting universal fact.

Indeed, this provides the ostensible basis for some of the most churlish exploration presently being done in the field. Philip K Dick, Marshall Hurk, JG Ballard, Jeff Lint and various other writers who deal fairly directly with psychological matters can yet be labelled writers of SF, for they explore the relationship between the human essence and the marshy (or not so marshy) landscapes through which the human spirit lurches.

Lint's special province has been attacks upon men by alien squid who are themselves bored with the entire undertaking, and the eventual agreement of bored man and bored squid to get on with something more fruitful. Under the reign of modern organization, this decision is alarming in establishing an individual and even viable world-view brought about by the admission of the obvious. In creating an overview of Lint's work I have assigned differently-colored jars of jelly in my head according to literary merit. This I have done in spite of a largely uncomprehending public, but the significance of Lint's work is such that I would do anything to dissipate the cloud of ignorance and bloody-minded no-can-do attitude which at this time prevents a wider appreciation of Chicago's least-known 'fiction hen' among readers.

PART 1: Jeff Lint and the Tentacled Beauty

ALTHOUGH IT IS often claimed that Lint is concerned with 'the spider of reality,' the assumption is usually that he is merely writing while half asleep or smashed on warm beer and drugs. Yet Lint is far from being the lethargy artist he is often considered. Lint's fiction is the equivalent of the knife-fingered ghoul which leaps upon one's chest at night and slashes away while screaming with laughter. Since at least Mary Shelley's time, science fiction has displayed a quite cheerful attitude toward mankind's resolve to render nature inoperative. The image of Frankenstein's monster, the creature born of science, that assumes a life of its own and threatens to kiss its creator on the eyes, still haunts today's world, where critics like Jem Egerton can argue that mental lethargy has assumed a life and logic of its own that puts it beyond human control. By the middle of the nineteenth century, even the hell-born visionary painter Jean-Claude Torrey could feel justified in puckering his lips a bit thoughtfully and painting the act in 'I For One Would Welcome a Bit of Steam' (1845).

Soon after this the theories of Darwin and Carnz were to lend new credence to the idea of blandly assumed change and rolling evasion. They pointed the way to the dead state; the inevitability of perfection was a notion well suited to the generally naive spirit of the times. But the subjugation of the environment marked the failure of imagination. By the end of the century the Victorian world had folded in upon itself, near to exhausted from Chinese underwear parties and bellicose grandstanding.

HG Wells' fin de siècle all-tentacle romances strikingly illustrate a rejection of the dominant order of mind. *The Time Machine*, peopled with winsome Eloi and boring Morlocks, and with its final consolatory vision of the end of the world, brought a measure of optimism. But it is in *The War of the Worlds* that Wells gave the world his funniest vision of mankind accosted by armored space squid. The image of Earth invaded by jellied eels from another world left beamish boys the world over praying to Mars rather than any deity. With all corners of this planet filled to overflowing with the filth of the human race, new hope must be found. Alien jelly is that hope, the tentacled beauty craved by mankind. The coming of the tentacled beauty is not a loss of innocence, but a desire fulfilled. The curiosity inspired by the being beyond suggests that if something genuinely interesting doesn't happen soon the sane among us will voluntarily extinguish our own consciousness. In fiction, and increasingly in the public mind, the gods and demons of yesterday have become the tentacled beauties of today.

If the image of the tentacled beauty plays so large a role in the fiction of Lint, it is because he deals always with the intelligent man's underwhelmed state; and it is the realization, often sudden and unexpected, of his disappointed condition that initiates the nervy but necessary struggle toward something of interest, however much this inconveniences the remainder of society.

When the common people of Earth are subjugated by incomprehensibly tyrannical new octopi in 'The Sky Deans,' Knut Royce seeks salvation in sleep. Who is to be punished and who is to escape the punishment/reward context depends on an individual's ability to 'angle off' of the given options. The bulging role of tentacled beauties in Lint's SF is to be understood in terms of the self's relation to the interesting but as yet unencountered. The tentacled beauty Donimo contacts Royce saying: 'I expected an enemy, not criminals happy to help. A vein of gold is liable to cause trouble, especially if it's in your arm.' It exhibits a vividness that lies beyond the societally human. Even when on familiar terms with humans, T-Bs are infused with an aura of colorful thoughtfulness and are thus associated with activities avoided by most humans. Thus not all tentacled beauties are friendly toward humans; some may yawn openly in their presence, and the ones with large mouths may snap up a human and swallow him or her before anyone can stop it, like the Wendts who come into conflict with humans in 'The Belly Cannot Lie.' In this story the inhabitants of Earth welcome extraterrestrial visitors with insincere, uncomprehended platitudes, dismal jokes and music. The tentacular visitors may be seen on occasion not only to vomit copiously, but also to become violent for the first time in their near-eternal lives.

Carl Jung has described flying-saucer sightings in terms of ladles and halved cherries reflected off the eyes of unusually large adult penguins. In 'Out of the Frying Pan and Straight to Video' Ron Nixon has written: 'The process of creating imaginary beings is in essence a process of mental economy, accomplishing a great deal literarily with a minimum of strokes. Whatever remains unfulfilled here can be compensated for in porn.'[5] In his study 'My Dust Is My Business' Plank contrasts the attitudes of Pascal and Kant toward the realm beyond Earth, noting how the contemplation of an empty universe inspires relief, while the thought of a space colonized by humans provokes dismal disgust.

Michael H. Hersh

In Lint's 'The Town Destroyer' the connection is made between alien jelly and the realm of the afterlife when what seems to be a star-nosed badger begins shouting at the protagonist. Typical of Lint is the fact that messages from beyond should announce themselves through a glossy mammal rather than any technological device. (Typical also of Lint is the fact that in this charming story the protagonist should wonder irritably if this repeated shouting is really necessary and whether it will upset his digestion.)

Beyond the dreary territory of normal human experience, then, is the undiscovered country that delights the curious. If the tentacular presence seems a manifestation of a lower order, it yet lies beyond unsatisfactory human dealings and is rarely boring to the fully sensory. This concept, which plays a prominent role in 'The Town Destroyer,' is made even more explicit and dramatically concise in 'Furioso,' where a space pineapple is portrayed as godlike, or at least utterly inhuman. This story, undoubtedly one of Lint's most conventional, is set in a future when democracy has triumphed over capitalism. Yet the patience of the human world is sorely tested by the arrival of the fruit. While somehow undermining their stable world, it does not move or speak. Though much of the public believes the pineapple to be sacred, one man eats it for breakfast with some bread. Thus it is suggested that the exhaustingly predictable polarization in the world that has supposedly been defeated, has in fact triumphed, though its triumph remains invisible to most because each views the situation from their own polarity. The fear of being a saint in a world of drab demons is similarly apparent in the relation of Parson Dibs and John Helicon in 'Furioso' and raises the question of Lint's recognition of the social weakness in honesty. The pineapple eater possesses only a fraction of a degree more individuality of thought than the worshippers, presenting no threat to the scheme of things. Only one glimpse is given of an actual individual—an unnamed woman who glides past Senator Brisby on a bicycle after the assassination, paying no mind to the security chaos.

The concept of the tentacled beauty, which makes its initial appearance pullulating out of the underhatch of a landed spaceship, is carried to its logical conclusion in the beauty of our inner tentacles, that is, the admission of our physical reality, or indeed any actual reality at all (an attitude almost unheard of today). It is Lint's compelling fusion of inner and outer tentacles which lends his work much of its power.

In 'The Enforced Amateurs' the least busy of the Rumidons, the tentacled beauties in the story, induces a sense of panic in those he confronts: facing bureaucrats, their qualities are exaggerated until they are not only incapable of action but unable to digest; facing the man on the street, the hapless, externally-origined man emerges, jittering on the spot and waiting for instructions which he now fears will never come. A child experiences a transjellyation of reality along the lines of a lucid dream: ordinary things, wherever she looks, seem to be getting more interesting.

Marshall Hurk's 'Snaggle Chops' provides another good example of the fusion of inner and outer tentacles. Scientist IG Farben, whose miscalculations have led to everyone growing a third eye and twenty-six ears, suffers from stress and the belief that he is to blame. And when he finds that prior to the incident he has invested massively in optometric and hearing-related technology, he suspects that at a subconscious level he must have planned the accident.

Many of Lint's stories illustrate his concern with the attempted maintenance of human relations at levels of being that are unable to maintain themselves without recourse to fashion and intrinsically valueless commerce. For Lint, the natural tendency of a species to strip itself of creative meaning is stultifying nightmare, and he sees the tendency everywhere, despite the steady accumulation of lustrous paintings of badgers in his own apartment.[6] In 'Hate Too Late' the erstwhile antagonist is the Understandably Uninterested Manticore;

in *Jelly Result* the maintenance of the dull order of the world occurs in a state of automated human patch-and-repair, where the systems repaired prey on the life force of its maintainers. Lint recognizes in human culture a collective death-wish, a longing for the ultimate eyes-open destruction or eternally sustained blandness foretold by subVedic mythology.

In 'Bless' Tommie Ochs awakes one morning to find that he has no tentacles, and must live by his wits from moment to moment. Dashing out into the world, he discovers that nobody else has any tentacles either, that they don't miss the lack of them and claim in bafflement never to have had any. Lint's metaphor points up a moral or ethical sensibility which, unheld and unrecognized by anyone else on the planet, is not communicable.

Throughout Lint's work there is this continual opening of the abyss, which partially informed the manifestos of the Vortical movement, which announced in its '1964 Declaration of Blamelessness' that it had proved to human beings 'how lovely our cheeks are, and on what unstable foundations they are based.' The presence of the abyss reveals Lint's position as fundamentally vortical. The individual divided from his cultural surroundings is likely to become increasingly aware of himself and his inner tentacles.

PART 2: Robot as Wallpaper

UNLIKE MANY OTHER SF authors, Lint has not bothered to put any cows in his published fiction. The early tale 'The Ghosts of a Zillion Slaughtered Cows' was never published, and he seems to have dismissed all cow fiction from then on. This shatters the statistical regularity of the cow's familiar presence in traditional SF. In a literature that has prided itself on rational extrapolation and shunned the chaos implicit in more lively animals, such a quantum leap into the unexpected strikes a note very close to heresy. Lint is not the first to understand the importance of a no-cow policy as a method of casting light on the possible. Wells understood implicitly that the real purpose of science fiction was not to describe globular, bone-idle black-and-white creatures who merely stare, occasionally batting their eyelashes. He refused to believe that cows stood at the nexus between man and his continually changing relationship with the world around him. Wells had no use for the juvenile, and ultimately boring, Gernsbackian preoccupation with cows-for-the-sake-of-cows; in his quest to tell mankind more about itself, his crazy mind showered the public with tales of tentacled beauty beings, animals transmuted into bait, inconvenience from outer space, alternative trousers, invisible hens, atomic blunder, early time and motion studies, and just about every other improbability so dear to later SF drudges. If science has been 'catching up' with science fiction in the interval, it is only to the extent that the field has tried too hard to be respectably 'all-tentacle.' The 'churlish maelstrom' posited by respectable astronomers, for instance, rests on a misconception of the sky, which is really only a piece of cheap velvet.[7] Yet even Wells maintained that the kind of fantasy he wrote should be based on a single bloody-minded premise: that he was the loveliest man on Earth. It was only by keeping the rest of the story as close to everyday reality as possible that he managed to get away with that central conceit.

Science fiction has generally been loath to stray far from the path prescribed by Wells. Not so Jeff Lint. Lint everywhere violates his readers with original thought. In fact, Lint generally goes out of his way to prevent the reader from liking anything he says. For Lint, the details of his own arms are fantastic. Lint is a pioneer of the 'post-cow ultra-tentacle meat explosion' anticipated by Robert E White.[8] Indeed, the 'six kinds of jelly necessary to fantasy fiction' delineated by Janet[9] are not in the least inconsistent with most of Lint's work, despite the fact that Lint specifically excludes 'elf jelly' from fantasy fiction thus defined.

What is the reader expected to do with such stories? In what context of rationally-explainable yet cowless reality are these worlds where people practice 'air kerning' and play 'ambulance trumpets'? Where 'Zerzan braces' are the units of currency for interplanetary trade, where a bendy elite undergo treatment by sleepy doctors who biologically lower people's expectations in an attempt to control the rate of evolution—these worlds where each day begins with the communal destroying of an interdimensional parasite which dangles titanically from the sky and appears anew each morning? And the man beside you on the ledge turns out to be a skinful of luminous doves?[10] Surely this universe, even before it is damped down by hallucinogenic drugs, is the place to be. Its dreamlike quality is accentuated by the silent stone fiends that gather on the corner of every block (so-called 'gargoyles'). When describing things Lint often selects the wrong detail, and leaves us to triangulate—sometimes for weeks or months at a time—until we locate the feature he was meaning to discuss. A mild example is his long description of the darkness which is gathered around the legs of Vermaxian toads and the fact that this makes it impossible for people to know what those limbs might look like. He forgets to explain that the darkness, extending to less than an inch from the surface of their legs, is caused by the pants they are wearing. In Lint's world Zurich, Switzerland, is indistinguishable from Marin County, California, because 'one head per fella' is the norm. The merging of the profound and the shambolic heightens experience in the manner of a lardy squire's first and cheapest opium dream. Lint's work is characterized by what Meek has called 'an almost out-of-control obsession with lobsters and their strange explanations'[11]—but it is the fact that Lint claims to have heard the lobsters' several and conflicting explanations for their behavior, that extends his work beyond mere enumerative naturalism to the muddy thinking of a zoological apologist. 'The water is our enemy' is no real excuse for lobsters to walk forward and forward, ever clacking their mittens. And Lint tries to gloss over the fact that only one motive is given for lobsters' all-one-color appearance, a feeble, vague claim that they are 'here to stay.'

It is a magic realism in which things are seen, done, and stared at for empty hours in the aftermath, emitting carbon dioxide. In the lunchtime chaos of accelerating dimensions it is pointless to ask what aspects are worth noticing. Diamond doors, suitcases that are found to be dead, jet failure over hell, dogs laughing in gangs—it is a world we all recognize, but if Lint's stories are filled with objects and processes that waste time, this is neither more nor less than we deserve.

The robot in Lint's science fiction is not a fab new toy with which to bash the hero, nor a symbol of human/slave relations, nor a glyph for exploring sentience definitions, but merely a pile of barely articulated bread. In its crappy morphology and functional uselessness, it assumes a role as symbolic human. It speaks in platitudes and offers no insights, as the reader quickly discovers.

Asimov's robots were simply chess-playing computers given human characteristics by authorial intervention. The robot is not a channel to the divine; unlike the tentacled beauty, it maintains an essential unity with the human in its lack of individual volition and complete availability to direction. Yet Whittemore, the hero of Lint's consciously Asimov-styled short 'The Robot Who Couldn't Be Bothered,' appears indistinguishable from other robots (and humans) until given an order—at this point it is discovered that his inactivity is the result of 'eleven million nodes of personal consideration.' Lint, too, appeared inconspicuous until ordered to do something—at which point, groin beware. 'Considering you're a robot,' says John Dessicant, 'I don't see why you shouldn't stun the pig of my choice.' The robot states, 'I already knew that you don't.' As usual, no actual question has been asked because there is no real desire to learn.

Lint's voice is remarkable for its lack of interest in anything standard-issue. His characters move through lies like smoke, rarely pausing to dignify them with a look. Even lacking a physical objective they move with truth in sight. Style reinforces anger in Lint's stories and what may appear as serious defects in style from one critical vantage become logical moves from another, depending on the reader's knowledge of history and power dynamics. Lint is unashamedly aware of these matters and his style is inextricably tied to his world-view, his conception of a mess of a planet lashed around with man-made chains. Indeed, Lint's works have been characterized by Lewis Tambs as 'Bitter Baroque': 'His protagonists traffic in casually relentless honesty in the face of four thousand years of layered lies and evasion strategy. They like an opportunity to do something confoundingly strange, but they prefer to have the rare-as-white-gold peace to get on with their own projects, and occasionally some jam.'

Lint's heroes, while they may delight some and baffle or annoy others, are characterized by a dismissively playful and fertile individuality, unencumbered by convention, and limited only by the strength in their legs.

In 'Woe Unto the Belly' for example, it is casually remarked of the hero: 'It was disappointing to her when Eddie floated into the room, seemingly thinking of something else, a faint frown on his face, knocking over a lamp.' Eddie's interesting levitation skills, the result of gargantuan effort and independence of thought over many years, are a mere baffling inconvenience to others.

Lint's disappointment at the wasted possibilities exemplified in the resolutely mediocre, and his suspicion of the motives of fear and evasion behind that resoluteness, make for strong and heady works. Those works belie his surface reputation as a balloon-folding moron whose works should be preserved 'in the furnace of history.'[12]

PART 3: Sacrifice

THOUGH LINT HAS grown more deadly and accomplished in his style over the years, thematically his fiction has remained fairly consistent. Even in an early short story like 'The Cobbler's Ordeal' he is concerned with erstwhile 'helper elves' which instead expect the cobbler to work for them. The cobbler finds that they will not believe or acknowledge his honest assertion that he will neither work for them nor expects them to work for him. He must finally lock these boring, one-note leeches in a cellar and flood it with boiling tar.

In 'Are You Joking' Professor Trickledown attempts to save people time and suffering by processing a number of truths into living jellies, the better to preserve them. But he and his peers cannot help but eat them immediately, and the professor is finally resolved to instead write the truths down so that future generations cannot ignore them. When he declares this intention a titanic blast of incredulous laughter explodes through the room, shattering his eardrums. Trickledown has made the one statement that the very facts of reality cannot help but respond to. More scorn is displayed in 'Pinhead Options,' in which the development of a self-organizing system animal is diverted just in time when it senses the qualities of humanity and resolves to become something entirely the opposite of mankind: a man. In Lint's landscapes we find a stinking ghetto of perspectives in which people and the world deserve each other.

Ted Abbey in 'Kenny's Dome' illustrates the megalomaniacal misuse of other people's time that leads to soul poverty and meaninglessness. "'Driver,'" Ted said, "I'll let you in on it. I'm playing the long con on you. I'm a bastard, like the President. I wasn't supposed to give the show away, but I can't go on with it quietly all the time. I'm just a law-writer, made out of dust held together by plastic blood. I'll never apologize, and knowing it won't help you without power, but it's a fact.'" Here the oppression is external in origin but its maintenance is internal and saturative, so the truth can be occasionally stated without causing a blip in the system. Lint does not intend to present a surface model of reality—a bureaucrat would never admit such truths to himself let alone others—but the verities stated in the story cause the surface to dissolve away. Whatever the links with external politics ('For each party to assume a different position, there must be enough lies to go around,') the focus for Lint is on subjective personal experience, the level of 'inner tentacles.' Thus at one point in 'The Cardiac Wall' the narrator can declare: 'It was my own tentacles which constricted me, not only the squid's. There was some fraction of power *granted* the enemy.' It appears to me that in this regard Meek fails to notice what he elsewhere so correctly points out: Lint's ability to transcend the 'space elf/exo-tentacle/cow-inclusive' drone of standard science fiction. In general it can be said that for Lint robots represent machines that are becoming even more boring, while androids represent humans whose only innovation is in their forms of boringness. Dorn of 'Thataway' is a 'status robot'—brisk dread on the surface, anxious dread beneath. His construction suggests he exists in a state half android and half robot, poised between the inauthentic and the artificial. Dorn realizes that by asserting control over his actions, which all his life have been directed by external fashion and too-close-to-see power-plays, he can take control of a few seconds of his life each day. Eventually Dorn gains enough power to cut his throat.

In Lint's universe, persons who manage to become separated from the society of their fellows have that much more hope of birthing an original thought or act. The failure of an individual to de-integrate himself from society as defined through learned cultural values results in the continued absence of his own perception of reality.

In 'The Venom Exchange' radically different arm and leg arrange-ments cause conflict between humans and tentacled beauties, each species seeing the other in a negative light, each able to perceive only a partial truth about the other, especially the waiters and head waiters of the different species. On the inter-personal or inter-societal level, the arguments and even physical clashes of waiters means the dissolution of culturally-conditioned behavior and the emergence of more 'primitive' and animalistic tendencies, often characterized by explosive outlets of sobbing, girlish screaming and catfight behavior among males. Holly Trent notes: 'Waiters are always, of necessity, emotionally fragile. Yet just as it is impossible for a man to build a matchstick boat while wearing boxing gloves, it is impossible to like a waiter.'[13] Humanity's belief in its need for waiters is not only perceptional, but spiritual, as it displays weakness and evasion in both realms. The haughty, even spooky detachment and preoccupation of the waiter reduces the diner's ability to experience a secure reality, but also serves as the vehicle for the expression of the diner's apparent reality—that he is being served. 'The measure of a man is not his intelligence. It is how many waiters he can disable within two minutes of entering a restaurant.' Thus spurts Jaen Amober, theoretician of the street in *I Blame Ferns*. His observations do not make him a better human being; he is shown still subject to all the old failures to deal properly with the world. It is only after he is seemingly stripped of their powers and reduced, outwardly, to the appearance of an underchef that we begin to understand his true path in life. He sacrifices his life for us, and thus helps us realize the importance of life and precisely directional disregard. 'The destruction of a million carrots, the transfer of political power—I understand these things,' Amober says before entering the rear of the restaurant. 'I know how it's wonderful. Pretty soon someone else will understand it, too. They must. Do you see?' The jolt provided by his donning the bib may in fact be required for such understanding.

This change in perspective is common to many of Lint's stories, and one that can be seen in as early a piece as 'Jack Rose.' The character around whom this story centers is 'A man from a planet which is exactly the shape of his head.' As tentacular ships invade the solar system, the protagonist of 'Again?' muses that 'you can tell they're some kind of octopi. You just can.' The tentacled beauties land in Arizona, thus unexpectedly catapulting its redundant functions into pole position. The hero realizes that he can move along the ground by squirming. 'I mean, let's face it; the octopi showed us how.' It is the coming of the unknown, the unexpected, the almost-interesting that confronts man with the possibility of such charmless locomotion.

Curly Weimar's solution to the apparent threat posed by the tentacled beauties in 'Fursaxa' is to crash his car through the windshield of their spaceship. 'His whole psychology, his point of orientation, revolved around different ways to crash his car. He loved it.' Dr. Rove, the doctor trying to mend Curly's bones, faces a crisis of his own, for he knows that without this central pastime Curly will be cast adrift in thought and uncertainty: hell for an American. Rove rescues himself and Curly from the grip of this dilemma by killing him. Being able to see beyond the structures of everyday control and yet determined to remain bereft of control of his being, the doctor must kill. But there is a price to be paid for taking a life: 'as long as he lived he would never regain the purity of his illusion of wanting to be free.'

The person who has been confronted with a sobbing, hysterical chef cannot return to the old unexamined life. At the end of 'Sam Doyle Amplified' Sam rediscovers, in stumbling upon two head waiters battling with flick-knives in a dirty alley in Tijuana, his own will to survive, and to find amusement in the struggle for survival. Shooting both waiters with a roof-mounted machine gun, he drives closer to the bodies to find any remaining life signs. 'I can see what you mean, sir,' one waiter chokes through bubbling blood. 'I can't endure reality as such. I have to have uniquely special conditions. God bless you, sir. I can see that you're a good man.'

Waiters are unusually prominent in Lint's stories. Not only are they numerous, but they are unusually aware and angry. Many are highly intelligent, and almost all are eventually found to be fiercely independent. In light of this situation, relations between men and waiters are never to be taken for granted—indeed, are often difficult, even desperate. 'Tectonic' is the outstanding example here: the tale of a frustrated dining experience and the need for authentic ingredients, it contains some of Lint's most poignant and effective writing. Whatever the roles of actual waiters, however, the concept of waiters symbolizes the potential for an edible plate of food. To quote Lint: 'The restaurant diner has only one true consolation, as he perishes: that he tried.'[14]

'Make It Quick' quite clearly makes this connection between waiters and the jaded hope for honest and fair exchange in life. The struggle between man and waiter rages through Lint's work. The diner's assumption of a tacit agreement between himself and his waiter is in some respects like Goethe's Faust, himself struggling against a flood. The waiter's eventual grim triumph, even if it cannot always be permanent, reveals to the diner the reality of affairs at this low rung of struggle. And though the meal is over, there are always glimmerings of new meals waiting, and so the lesson is unlearnt in the hope of a better experience in future—thus hope repels wisdom. If corruption touches all the works of humankind, and the body itself must disintegrate, why is the idea of waiters' evil so unacceptable to man? It is perhaps the fact of manipulation not by an over-arching authority but by one's fellow-man, or even one who should be serving (in itself a nightmarish reminder of the smirkingly stated intention of government to serve the people). The setting for 'Honeysun' is a world without waiters, chefs or pasta, a world where everyday objects become so filled with joy that they spring up and 'celebrate' by flushing through with bands of rainbow neon. Matt Valentine finds his whole house celebrating in this manner: 'I got in to the apartment after trying eleven times to unlock the door—the keyhole kept spurting spunk over my hand.' 'Yes,' the house tells him, 'by making use of the most advanced techniques of present-day science, I can spurt spunk over your hand, and at a price any apartment owner can afford! I love you I love you I love you! It's a wonderful world!' Valentine, who had imagined himself to control his world, is forced to admit that he feels pretty dismal about everything.

Lint does not always hesitate to postulate the possible existence of a phantom waiter. In Plato's allegory of the cave, the realm of waiters exists outside, but it is only their shadows, cast by an unseen source of light onto the cave wall, that erstwhile diners inside can see. 'The waiter isn't coming—the waiter is *dead*!' says one of the characters in 'Send For the Waiter.' Here people abdicate their positions as non-productive actors in human evasion and attempt to leave the restaurant with decisive dignity. '"You want this knife?' Corsano asked. '*Take* it. No waiters, no chef, no manager—let's *take* whatever we want.' His voice rose with hysteria. 'Let's see them emerge from wherever they're hiding and try to *stop* us!'" They set light to the restaurant and crash out through the windows with their swag. 'We'll keep it all—not to prize as a reminder, but to use, every day. You can't grasp the difference now, but you will.' Behind them, the startled and vacillating restaurant staff have only just emerged into view. The knives and forks represent the ideal state which is to be aspired to, the imperfect but possible world of public dining, and the forces of abuse, neglect and manipulation which dominate when waiters abandon paying customers.

Lint is concerned both with man's relation to man and with man's relation to power structures. Human beings find themselves part of an exploitative machine which adds insult to injury by being boring. For an illusion of a free world to convince for any length of time, the system projected should at least function theoretically, and this is where the current illusion fails. Luckily, the Earth is 'packed with morons.' In 'Packed With Morons' we are shown a moron apparently thinking, but clearly mistaking other people's thoughts for his own. So it does not surprise us that, when asked for his thoughts on a certain matter, he produces the desired response.

As his lower body is constricted and flayed in an industrial mincer and his torso begins to follow, our hero has the glimmering realization that he has made a sacrifice, but merely uses the puzzling fact as firm-chinned justification for what he is doing, even as that chin is unwound like an apple. Lint's heroes are rarely such ordinary folk. The characters that populate Lint's fantasies are, by and large, individuals—and what they make of their lives depends to a very large degree on how far they can remove themselves from the norm. 'Exile is relief disguised as penance.' [*I Blame Ferns*]

1. Albert Camus, 'Clubbing the Guard and Loving It,' (*Youthful Writings*, Random House Inc, 1978)
2. Brandon Carr, 'Tentacles and Jam; and More Tentacles,' (*Species of Heart*, St Matthew Destiji, 1979)
3. Brandon Carr, 'Lint, Dick and the Downward Spiral,' (ibid)
4. Giles T Hatton, 'Hackin' Through Bracken,' (*Go Spacky Magazine*, 1978)
5. Ron Nixon, 'Out of the Frying Pan and Straight to Video,' (1984)
6. 'Out of What?,' *Rolling Stone*, 1972
7. Keith Connelly, 'Don't Blame Me,' (Harcourt, Brace & World, 1967)
8. Robert E White, 'Hooked On the Sky: Fiction Withdrawal in Vortical Literature,' (in Tobe Dilloway ed., *SF: The Other Side of My Face* (Dublin University Popular Press, 1971)
9. My wife Janet defines the six kinds of jelly necessary to fantasy

fiction as: alien jelly, robot jelly, spaceship jelly, elf jelly, big woman jelly and sad loser jelly.

10. Jeff Lint, 'Only In Miniature,' (1962)

11. Aaron Meek, 'The Fabric Shredder: Lint Blows Out in *The Stupid Conversation*,' (*Module Boot* No. 16, September 1977)

12. Jean Baudrillard, 'I Kiss the Furnace of History; It Does Not Respond,' (1979)

13. Holly Trent, 'Cognition and Estrangement: the Mannequin and the Waiter,' (*The Tone Won't Lower Itself*, Routledge, 1979)

14. Interview, *Pervader Zine*, 1977

Jeff Lint's 'Snail Camp'

Steve Aylett

MOST OF US have wondered at one time or another what the appeal of Jeff Lint's work is. The same strengths of his works are cited again and again by enthusiastic readers—a tribute to the consistency of his talent. That Lint is a builder of monsters so pointless and detailed that one could almost strangle him for wasting our time, this is obvious. That he is a master of exposing quite different human weaknesses than are normally dealt with in fiction or anywhere else, so different that he must often invent a new term for the failing (eg. 'cren'), is a matter of record. That he is a tentacle-obsessive who is simultaneously exhausted and scampering, tubby and lean, welcome and inconvenient; that he creates characters that display an unrealistically high level of combustibility, to the point that they will explode into flame when a match is merely shown to them, to those of us who read his novels and short stories this is no revelation.

What draws us into the worlds that Lint creates are his wayward protagonists. Certainly they are baleful and, far from being unassailable supermen, are often asleep, not easily awoken with a single shake, and sometimes given to throttling those who attempt it. In some books (eg. *Fanatique*) the protagonist will disappear for several pages while the book goes on, and then re-enter it without any explanation of where he's been (probably asleep or saying halloo to a dog). These heroes and heroines are a parallel breed: their motivations are obvious to themselves and alien to the average reader. Through Lint's pen we watch already strange characters become increasingly vivid individuals who are so much their own creature that when the crux of a certain social/ scientific/cosmic matter occurs, they are elsewhere doing something far more interesting and barely aware of the fashionable crisis. They would be the last to put effort into deciding the fates of others, as the worlds and societies around them are quite insincere about desiring to change. On the rare occasion that a Lint hero does change something ('An Ominous Mirth') everyone protests, agitated and embarrassed, because when they said they wanted the change made they assumed it was impossible. For the Lint hero, unlike the heroes of ancient myth, the unavoidable confrontation with his own nature occurs at the beginning or before the story starts, and he is first discovered sitting on the burning shell of a car, wearing some sort of seaweed bonnet and playing a lute. Even the mimsy and ineffective Alan Jay is first seen riding a tiger shark up an embankment and doing a double forward-flip into a barbecue to which he was not invited.

We find a fine Lintian hero in Benny Mena. Benny, the protagonist in the tale 'Snail Camp' (first published in pulp mag *Baffling Stories*), spends his young years in an oppressive environment. He must eat nine hundred snails every day, including the shells, and have his performance rated according to criteria that nobody understands. Unbeknownst to his friends and colleagues in Snail Camp, he has learnt the snails' language and must endure their screams and entreaties. Though comfortable, existence in Snail Camp is dreary and mindless. There is no discussion of travel, growth or discovery; in

Benny's world such things are considered mere fripperies, the musings of a spooky and selfish child. Benny attempts to find out whether, if he stops eating snails or perhaps eats them in a 'sarcastic' way, he will be merely banished or actually punished. To find out, he knocks out a colleague and accuses him of sleeping, then places a snail 'spy' on the boy's back. The boy is taken away and, several months later, the snail returns saying that the boy was perversely rewarded by banishment. The hero falls asleep, is banished, and later returns with a neutron bomb.

It might be said that 'Snail Camp' is a standard-issue everyman tale, showing the too-close-to-see manipulations in our work-a-day existence, where nothing new is permitted and yet truth is simultaneously deplored as a pre-colonized territory. But Benny presents us with a more optimistic picture of ourselves: a chubby moron who stumbles through existence until the facts bite off part of his nose. Herein lies the essence of a true hero, the kind that Lint so easily creates, be it Felix Arkwitch or Valac of the novel *Jelly Result*. As Lint scholar Eileen Welsome has said, 'Seeing the underpinnings of the world at all times, he finds himself to be terribly frank and unpopular wherever he goes.' Lewis Tambs has described Lint's fiction as 'Bitter Baroque': 'His protagonists traffic in casually relentless honesty in the face of four thousand years of layered lies and evasion strategy. They like an opportunity to do something confoundingly strange, but they prefer to have the rare-as-white-gold peace to get on with their own projects, and occasionally some jam.' Surge Brunner of Lint's novel *I am a Centrifuge* must make such constant allowances while moving through society's vacuum of evasion that he is effectively using his own skull as a sort of space helmet. That character too demonstrates the combination of obtusely-timed lethargy and pyrotechnical effrontery that makes the Lintian hero so inaccessible and appealing to his readers.

And Your Point Is?

In the words of Benny Mena as he watches the obliteration of Snail Camp, 'If all governments were combined, we could save on travel and gunpowder.' Accusation or guidebook to cultural delight? You decide.

'The Horizon Through the Buttonhole'

by Jeff Lint
(set text module US 1996)

SET TEXT SUMMARY

The reader is shown a manhole in which a fizzing darkness proves to be a wormhole into vast quantities of spare time. A very old, withered clown emerges and grabs the leg of a passerby, cracking the man's head on the concrete. The passerby demands, amid a scorching volley of abuse, what the bastard thinks he's playing at. The clown's response is a flashback that forms the rest of the story.

Caleb Marx, Chief Traffic Controller for the insect world, had a big problem. The mosquitoes of South America are failing to die, so that some had now lived for twenty or more years, the build-up resulting in vehicle crashes and sarcastic riots. Having exhausted all other solutions he turns to Ken User, an inventor who lives in a private hell.

Afflicted with a mind of his own from earliest childhood, Ken lacks the immorality to lie or to justify hurting people with his arms and legs. By living in a weighted sphere of honesty he is able to live unharassed, as the orb is designed to seem quite uninteresting from the outside, and unfashionable always from any angle. His primary invention is a herd of uncontrollable barnyard animals which the authorities want captured dead or alive. These mechanical monsters—even the sheep—have glittering steel fangs almost a foot long, and whisper the word 'default' en masse, so that the word has become known as a really classic spooky omen of imminent death.

Caleb contacts Pam Galloway, one of Ken's few friends, who agrees to take him to see the inventor. Pam has a mechanical herd of her own: some giant spiders, each with an abdomen the size of a coconut. These things are so heavy they can't really move up walls or scuttle very fast, but are nevertheless of exactly the correct size and proportions to damage everyone's long-term mental health. Pam expects Caleb to take a professional interest in the spiders, but Caleb merely humors her and is clearly bored. During their visit, Ken tells Pam he will work on both problems—that of Caleb's ennui and the bug longevity—eventually deciding incorrectly that the two issues are related.

Ken learns that a land surveyor, Jack Parsons, has been able to kill a dozen mosquitoes, apparently by magic. Ken asks the surveyor his secret. Parsons, it turns out, is a dry husk.

Ken decides finally to channel all living bugs through a wormhole into an alternative universe, leaving only his own and Pam's artificial animals to thrive. In foodchain terms he has 'kicked them upstairs,' observing with satisfaction that it should give them 'alot of action.' Caleb, exasperated at Ken's irresponsible act, follows the true bugs through the wormhole into our own world, where twenty years in the other dimension is equivalent to a mere three days. But, having lost track of the movements of at least ninety million of his 'targets,' Caleb lurks at the entry point of our world to intercept any through-traffic, of which there has been none for sixty-two years.

Baffled and impatient at Caleb's explanation for grabbing his leg, the passerby kicks him in the mouth. As the passerby walks away, Caleb hangs painfully sideways from the manhole and shouts after him: 'Ignorance of the past is a major theme throughout history; and the gap between the powerful, stupid men of the past and the powerful, stupid men of the present and future is starkly evident when the characteristics of ancient empires are held up against those of present empire.'

Despite what is clearly meant to be an enigmatic coda to the story, the passerby hears the remark and turns around, stalks all the way back to the manhole and kicks Caleb again, knocking him unconscious.

COMMENTARY by Alex Vasconi, aged 12, Case School, Florida
THIS STORY CHANGED my life by showing that insects and manhole clowns aren't all scary, and can have problems of their own. I especially liked the scene with the sheep, that literally 'bite the hand that feed them.' The spiders werent all that frightening, as it was obvious you could kill them with a normal hammer. The Ken character was a bit stern, but we could see he was trying. It was not a surprise that the clown became Caleb; anyone could see it a mile away. We are not sleeping.

Sadly Disappointed

George Cane

ONE COULD CLASS Lint with the 'resolute but charmless' authors so skillfully dismissed by Larry Hagman but Lint is a writer who achieves his own brand of charm. With a few exceptions, such as the editorially butchered *One Less Bastard* (what's with the boulder?), his themes, plots, and characters tend to merge into a device-rich complexity of mischief which, more so than the plot, leave a hypervivid impression of Lintian contempt. Panicky explanations to pursuers, desperate but exasperatingly uninventive bids for absolution, hallucinations less interesting than actuality, vicious Chinese women, and disconcertingly fragile insects appear so casually as to give one the feeling of some accusation of mediocrity at the cellular level. Nor am I unsure that this is not a truthful depiction of Lint's struggle with society—a constant attack on an obsessive theme, expressed with every imaginative device he can lay his stupid hands on, but leading at last to the same impression of casually ascended derision.

But there are Lint novels—fewer than two—of less clarity and less individuality. An example is *Sadly Disappointed*.

When I first read it I thought it more broad than most Lint

93

works. Later it occurred to me that it was an 'experiment' in grafting SF onto the 'satanic possession' novel, and there certainly is a deal of such hokey characterisation, ritual and plotting in it. I could only recall the various muttered, embarrassed conversations of the priests sent to deal with the supposedly possessed child in question, who has turned out to be perfectly normal and not possessed by anything interesting at all.

So I re-read it, and a different book emerged. *Sadly Disappointed* is, believe it or not, a novel about family—and a very bad one. But it is interesting and, though crap, is worth the attention of someone like you.

The parents in the story have a typical love-hate relationship with their son, Timmy. A typical six-year-old, he stands at some psychological remove from the rest of humanity and is more spooky than cute. His remarks and expressions are fixed and merciless. (This may be the book's first symbol of the more usual Lint stance).

He is hospitalized after an attack by a small, crazy dog and wakens to find himself healed but surrounded by exorcists whom his parents have summoned in a desperate bid to make him special. He becomes fodder for the contemporary possession fashion, thrust into the common world he does not understand. His parents throw jelly over him when nobody is looking, and then claim to have seen the child ejecting ectoplasm from the front nozzle of his face.

And nobody—literally nobody—believes his parents' story. The priests do not believe them, nor do their friends, lawyer, etc. The hoped-for controversy never gets off the ground.

His parents finally return to their practice of trying to shock the neighbors with 'revolutionary' practices such as gonk-burning, wearing acapulco shirts and talking about 'air monkeys.'

At this point we learn that Satan does not exist, in an administrative sense; there is no real documentation of him anywhere in the world. Timmy's parents spend the rest of the novel in 'trun,' Lint's term for the stiff chin-thrusting stance adopted upon having almost to admit a mistake.

And that's all that happens. Dumbest thing I ever read. I read it, I'm sure of that much.

This is Lint at his worst. The main trouble is that none of the characters are really Lintian anyway: none of them innovate, nor demonstrate the potential for true individuality.

An epilogue tells, lazily, what became of all the major characters, and the final paragraph, dealing not with a person but with an artifact, is worth quoting: 'That night a garbage truck defiantly continued living, taken over by the virgin suspicion that its body was its own and its own throne.' Thus the book ends as it seems about to spark interesting.

It is a boring novel—unentertaining, uninventive. It is not a good novel because the story, foreshadowing boring failure and then showing it, diverts attention from anything worthwhile we might be doing.

Recently *Nearly Eldritch* magazine debated Lint, with that reluctance to see much fault in his work which is the attitude of Lint fans in general. He was praised for (1) the inventiveness of his writing, (2) surrealism of character motivation, and (3) philosophy (Lintism?).

None of this is evident in *Sadly Disappointed*, an appropriately-titled book.

[Editor's Note: again, I emphasise that Lint did not write *Sadly Disappointed*; the author was Alan Rouch, perhaps attempting something of a Lint impersonation by borrowing his friend's 'pragment' terms such as 'trun' and 'lempy.')

Stating it Plain in
The Riding on Luggage Show

Dennis Ofstein

In Jeff Lint's three musicals (*Deft Accountancy, A Team Becomes Embers Together* and *The Riding On Luggage Show*) the audience was constantly threatened with real danger, whether in the form of poisonous jumping spiders, out-of-control fire, or wolves. They never really had the option of sitting back and letting the experience roll over them, as what inevitably rolled over them was toxic smoke. No finely-tuned aesthetic taste or social conscience could reconcile this when confronted with locked doors. More so in his plays than in his books, Lint found the relatable abhorrent, and the glee with which he sustained audience bewilderment was termed 'carnagio' (the energy of collapse too long resisted). Actors no longer had to worry about looking blank or smirking at odd moments, or even reciting from the wrong play—Lint would encourage his actors to select different scripts and run them concurrently on stage, creating strange dramatic intersections. (A performance combining *27 Workshy Slobs, The Ravaged*

Face of Saggy Einstein and *Blame the Moth* was billed as *27 Ravaged Moths*.)

In Lint's musicals, characters begin singing only when their resentment becomes too intense for speech—which is often. Lint subordinated every aspect of the play to his characters' resentments and these are anatomized in excruciating detail: 'A dollar I gave /for forty-nine cents/And fifty returned /so I was incensed /The cops did not care /to listen to fact/It always is so, /so with gun I act' ('Almost A Thousand Injustices Per Day Demanded This Retribution So Why Act Surprised,' from *Deft Accountancy*).

However, Lint apparently saw himself as someone who enjoyed and was good at working in theatre. It was supposed to be a form of cathartic entertainment, yet Lint's musicals satisfy the vortical mentality: they are fertile with 'creative resentment.' He is the Id of the musical.

In *The Riding On Luggage Show* he combined classical music, 'lurch ballet,' cattle rustling and straight theatre seamlessly. Many of the great musicals focus on a conflict between an individual and a community but in *Luggage* the entire cast seem to admire the Harp Shrike, a terrifying catgut devil with ribbed strings extruded from its chest which it plucks as blasts of wind and sodium-drenched light rip through its rags; the ultimate outsider. It is left to the play's audience to provide conflict, as they scream or crawl appalled from this onslaught of elements. Lint created a text that was unsettling only to those who are unaware enough to be 'settled' in the midst of the world's nightmare.

The plot is communicated mostly without dialogue, which has given way to gestures of gale-force glee. There is no attempt to separate law, vengeance, lighting, apocalypse, execution, murder or stage decor. Five times the action stops for blood tests. Many of the more hectic dances were performed without music or apparent choreography, a chaos which led members of the audience to shout out 'She's killing him!', 'Call the police!' or 'Won't somebody help that man?' These rituals of scorn entertained without patronizing the audience. *Luggage* never pretended to be an alternative to reality and had obvious links to Genet's *The Screens*. It does, however, suggest repeatedly how boring the audience is, and how they are proving themselves worthy of the scorn being heaped upon them. 'You are little piggies a-dangle over soup/Of your own creation!' sings the young, hale and hearty Mattlewire in the village square, surrounded by glaring citizens. Never before had the musical tackled such a sensitive subject. Mattlewire's flushed hilarity and his tendency to spring about are incredibly annoying. Once someone fired a gun at the stage during his 'I am all a-caper' scene, injuring a young Kevin Kline. Lint stood offstage urging him to 'Just keep laughing! Grin like an idiot!' Kline has followed his advice to this day.

Described as a toxic deathwish musical, *Luggage* was an innovation of its time. It was a kinetic condemnation, not a story, and surely intended to provoke. Throughout much of the play Lint seems to be asking the audience 'What the hell are you doing? Why have you come here? Don't you have anything better to do? Do I have such power or do you have so little? Are we powerless together?' And in the finale, the entire cast (riding in circles on some luggage—finally!) sing the infamous 'What the hell are you doing?' song, as its lyrics 'What the hell are you doing? Why have you come here? Don't you have anything better to do? Do I have such power or do you have so little? Are we powerless together?' are revealed on the backdrop in titanic, chiselled lettering—all taboo questions in previous musicals.

Then Mattlewire walks onstage with a large barrel, drops it to the floor, removes the lid and negligently shoves it over onto its side, walking off as thousands of poisonous jumping spiders pour from the stage and infest the theatre. Stories are still told of the screaming free-for-all provoked by the spiders, and inevitably the recent revival of the show saw the lethal creatures replaced with a barrel of tired, harmless garter snakes.

Because of its irreverence and in-your-face attitude *Luggage* was received unfavorably by both critics and audiences alike. It tested musical stage conventions and salted the soil so densely that anyone purporting to do anything interesting in the future had to pretend that *Luggage* had never happened. It proved that escapism was popularly regarded as preferable to social questions and that an audience confronted with honesty will almost always run away.

Belligerently Naked in Jeff Lint's 'The Retrial'

Jean-Marie Guerin

IN ORDER TO address the irritating lack of paradox in Lint's 'The Retrial' it is important to recognize the ongoing theme of ecstatic disregard (in the classic 'bailing out nude' sense). Without this undercurrent of beatific irreverence it is impossible to pin down Lint's Joseph K's complete lack of need or desire to become involved with the processes of oppression. It should be noted also that the 'berserk stenographer' style in which Lint relates the story is important in allowing these situations to actually appear less philosophically interesting than they are.

A central issue in K's dealings with memo-level fascism is that he often goes among people that will ignore or tolerate him or be merely baffled by him in some way. It could be to alleviate boredom and supply entertainment (Franz), to pass the time (the Chief Clerk), to lick his nose (Benji the Dog), to allow him time to build a preliminary sub-structure to further antics (Wolfart), and/or tell him what should be happening with his case were he paying attention and/or cooperating (Titorelli). In fact, K even seems to reflect on this when he first starts kicking the outer wall of the Usher's cabin.

"'I'm naked," he thought, almost amazed: "First being born, and now this. No trousers for me."' This realization does not seem to bother him, only cause him to wonder at the coincidence. To the reader however, especially after a second reading, this fact stands out as one of the greater questions of the story: how are these trouserless states related to K's caper through the court? How are they implicated in the proceedings and to what degree? What is their significance to K?

The naked role that K takes on is stated in the 'Long Hall try' scene when K 'thought for a moment of running faster, perhaps persuading someone to join him without notice.' Although this is not something he acts upon, it is clear that he at least occasionally wishes that others would act as he does.

Benji the Dog seems to be the only person that K gives serious thought to, and the reader is left wondering exactly what it is that he wants from Benji. Could it be purely physical? Could it be separate from the trial's proceedings? He treats Benji quite differently than he does Huld. For example Lint uses descriptive language to describe Benji's appearance and funny actions to a greater degree than he does when Hastert is introduced. The word 'glossy' is uncharacteristically used. Hastert does, on the other hand, tell K that he will be working at a law office and wants to help him. K's response—a sort of keening wail as 'snail-like antlers' appear from the top of his head—is mild compared to later outbursts. Hastert's importance to K is thus immediately one of forewarning, as K gets a bearing on the level of insult to be paid him by authority. The character of Hastert represents the Court in its bland assumption of deference, its automated and thus unimaginative provocation, and its lack of sense.

Franz is quite a standard Lint character. He just happens to be the lawyer's knifegrinder and is conveniently there to meet K. He is fishlike not only in his looks ('he had a gilled, carp-like face, his pale cheeks and chin forming a halfmoon which made temples and forehead unnecessary') but in his actions also. For instance, he gets K's attention by stropping a razor against the wall and laughing while regarding K with 'eyes like raisins.' In this sense he has some traits which are sympathetic with K, yet seems at other times to want to hamper him by giving him advice and information about the judges. His need and desire for K's (and others') regard is weak, as he states later that he thinks these people inferior. K can do without him, but it does seem that Franz provides respite from the lawyer's long speeches on the nonsensical judicial system. For example, 'the only welcome interruption during these visits was Franz, who always knew how to arrange things so that he sharpened a knife in K's presence. Then he would stand on a table.'

In discussing the role of belligerent nudity the scenes with Franz and K are excellent examples. They represent a 'hierarchy' of effrontery, a barely discernible theme which runs through this tale. It may appear that K is the only one to show rebellion in the face of meaningless law, but it is actually a credit to the character that his skyriding audacity puts even the 'spurting trumpet' antics of Wolfart in the shade. (Wolfart's behavior, which Wolfart believes shockingly confrontational, blends entirely with the bureaucratic background.)

It can be argued that all of these characters were secretly supportive of K, even to the point of plotting behind his back. Yet support which is not acted upon is not support.

Sources:
Cheerful When Blamed—Jeff Lint (Rich & Cowan, 1957)
The Trial—Franz Kafka
'The Bartleby Stance'—Simon Posford (*The Lintian* #7, 1995)

Lint's Intent

Steve Aylett

DENNIS OFSTEIN HAS stated (in regard to *The Riding On Luggage Show*) that 'anyone purporting to do anything interesting in the future had to pretend that *Luggage* had never happened.' An extension of this is that Lint fans, upon commencing the reading of subsequent authors' work, will usually begin by forgiving such authors their trespasses. Some have suggested that this attitude of forgiveness was the pinnacle of Lint's intention and that he may have been, like Jonathan Swift, one of the thirty-six 'hypocrites reversed' that appear in each generation. That Lint should ambush his readers into magnanimity through so tortuous a route seems unlikely to other observers—wasn't it his desire merely to accost us without taking the trouble to physically seek us out?

Lint knew that his use of originality as the basic building unit of a book would result in the perception of at least two different versions of the book among readers—the bifurcation would begin with readers who accepted and included diversity, and those who deemed difference an exception which need not be factored in. The first would perceive richness, the second emptiness, and perceptual graduation in between and beyond would aggregate from there. Thus Lint brought not peace, nor a sword, but a dicer. Or, more accurately, he revealed the varied prejudices of perception that already existed.

As Lint's character Boris Nadler says in 'Bonus/Bone,' 'When you plan to kill someone, you grant that person a great deal of influence over you.' In exploring and delineating the toxic world, the satirist is poisoned by it. The illusion that the understanding of hell will cause one's deliverance from it presupposes that knowledge is power; or that an overseeing power approves knowledge and rewards it. Inevitably, as an honest man and fugitive from conjecture, Lint was defenseless. (Satire has no effect—a mirror holds no fear for those with no shame.) What, then, did that leave him? Devoutly human but living the faith in his own way, with the chronic tendency to default to his own reasoning (not yet a crime at his time of writing), he became true north for clear-eyed resenters. He was a cure drug, a literary Ibogaine. But after doing the cure, you're on your own.

Lint was so critical of the world that even today biographers cannot explain how he could stand to live here. The mesmeric bitterness of his satire was deep enough to treat the awkwardness when two or more social pantomimes overlap; the fact that, if there hasn't been a war for a while, we're nearer to the next one than the last; and to make us accomplice in his honesty. Who would be cruel enough to tell the young that the world will not end? Yet even Lint was unprepared for newer generations who, upon reaching the end of a sentence, have forgotten the beginning of it. To them Lint's desire to make it through the media with facts intact—so well portrayed in the fluctuating geographies of his story 'Morning Edition Map'—can seem like plaintive cries from a graveyard of still-working formulas buried by accelerated style change. They haven't the attention to glimpse a truth which has only just synchronized with human language, and only briefly.

Appalled amid a literature which had become a ghost of itself, Lint created sentences which do not qualify or repent and are visibly singed by their re-entry from another realm. His transgression describes lines as subtly immaculate as those perfected by the waiter who swerves to avoid your eye—and her eye—and theirs—forever. Lint's habit of turning up on the wrong side of the ambush led embarrassed critics to suggest his genius was mistaken, a saint's headache. Yet his sentences have substances stored in their roots that will be released only after time. More than one reader has witnessed green-gold flukes opening in the page before clenching their eyes and looking again at innocent print. Truth, existing everywhere, can attack from any point—even from within your own body. Few today will accept the affliction of reality and few venture into the Lintian light without a shield against knowledge which, like rain, falls at an angle.

And Your Point Is?

'The Retrial' by Steve Aylett; first published in *Interzone* 198, 2005.

'Review of *I am a Centrifuge*' by Eileen Welsome; first published 1998 in *FlirtingWithMcCoy.com*.

'Redemption and ordeal in Jeff Lint's "Broadway Crematoria"' by Arkhipov Halt; excerpt from dissertation, 2004, Wayne State University.

'Give, Take and Take: An examination of Jeff Lint's "The Crystalline Associate" (collected in *Lint: a Collection*)' by Daniel Guyal; first published in *Too Pleased To Apologize Zine*, #14, Spring 1987, pp. 11; Detroit, US.

'The Lintian Waiter in "Tectonic"' by Chris Diana; first published in *Against Advice*, *The Caterer Fanclub Newsletter*, issue 17, 1998.

'Stress and Spillover in Three Lint Plays' by Steve Aylett first appeard in *Bust Down the Door and Eat all the Chickens*, issue 3, 2005.

'"Deep Vanishing" in Jeff Lint's Science Fiction' by Alfred Bork, Portland State University (Portland, Oregon), dissertation excerpt, 2003.

'"Rise of the Swans": Doing Bird With Jeff Lint' by Steve Aylett; first published in *fantasticmetropolis.com*, 2005.

'Inconvenience From Outer Space' by Michael H. Hersh; first published in *Sensurround Blame Magazine*, issue 14, 1985.

'Jeff Lint's 'Snail Camp" by Steve Aylett, first published in *The Idler* 35, 2005.

'Sadly Disappointed' by George Cane; from *Too Pleased To Apologize Zine*, #11, Summer 1986, pp. 18; Detroit, US.

'Belligerently Naked in Jeff Lint's "The Retrial"' by Jean-Marie Guerin; extracted from a paper, 'Jeff Lint: Bounty Spoken,' *Journal of Vortical Literature*, Issue 13, 1997.

About the Editor

Steve Aylett was born in Bromley, England. He left school at 17 and worked in a book warehouse, and later in law publishing, where he invented the concept of 'fractal litigation,' whereby the flapping of a butterfly's wings on one side of the world results in a massive compensation claim on the other. His first book *The Crime Studio* was generally regarded as a cry for help. This was followed by *Bigot Hall*, *Slaughtermatic*, *The Inflatable Volunteer*, *Toxicology*, *Atom*, *Shamanspace*, *Only an Alligator*, *The Velocity Gospel*, *Dummyland*, *Karloff's Circus*, *LINT*, and *Fain the Sorcerer*. He was a finalist for the 1998 Philip K Dick Award (for *Slaughtermatic*) and recently won the Prix Jack Trevor Story (or Jack Trevor Story Memorial Cup). The award is given for a work of fiction or body of work which best celebrates the humorous spirit of Jack Trevor Story, who died in 1992.

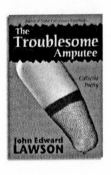

Printed in the United Kingdom
by Lightning Source UK Ltd.
116547UKS00001B/127-150